FLAMETHROWER

MAGGIE ESTEP

FLAMETHROWER

A RUBY MURPHY MYSTERY

 THREE RIVERS PRESS • NEW YORK

All rights reserved.
Published in the United States by Three Rivers Press,
an imprint of the Crown Publishing Group, a division
of Random House, Inc., New York.
www.crownpublishing.com
Three Rivers Press and the Tugboat design
are registered trademarks of Random House, Inc.

Library of Congress Cataloging-in-Publication Data
Estep, Maggie.
Flamethrower : a Ruby Murphy mystery / Maggie Estep.— 1st ed.
(alk. paper)
1. Women detectives—New York (State)—New York—Fiction.
2. Coney Island (New York, N.Y.)—Fiction. I. Title.
PS3555.S754F63 2006
813'.54—dc22   2006003885

ISBN-13: 978-1-4000-8273-5
ISBN-10: 1-4000-8273-0

Printed in the United States of America

Design by Lynne Amft

10 9 8 7 6 5 4 3 2 1
First Edition

To Andrew Vachss

ACKNOWLEDGMENTS

THANKS TO Dr. Ira Jaffe for the surgical tome and Steven Crist for probable fictional payouts, Yaddo and The Virginia Center for the Creative Arts for peaceful places to work, my brothers Jon and Chris Murray for reading early drafts, Jenny Meyer and Elizabeth Tisdale for the same, my valiant agent Tracy Brown for putting up with my shenanigans, and, always and forever, my partner in crime, John Rauchenberger.

FLAMETHROWER

1. LEG

If the day had been any brighter, it would have exploded. Ruby pushed her five-dollar sunglasses so far up the bridge of her nose that her eyelashes smashed against the lenses. This didn't help. She still felt invaded. Seemed like post-Giuliani Manhattan just kept getting garishly brighter, like the whole damn town was ready to blow.

Ruby stood tapping her foot against the sidewalk in front of the doctor's office. The Psychiatrist was uncharacteristically late, and Ruby started hoping Dr. Jody Ray had forgotten their appointment. Two more minutes and Ruby would gladly give up and go home to Coney Island, where, in spite of the bawdy amusement park and the broadness of sky over ocean, Ruby didn't need sunglasses even when walking on the beach at high noon.

Today wasn't a hot day. Anything under 80 and Ruby, who speculated that her personal genetic code was less removed from that of lizards than most people's, tended to get a chill. This day, weighing in around 75 degrees, was bearable but not the kind of bordering-on-tropical heat that made Ruby feel good all over. She was barely warm enough in a red halter-top and jeans.

Ruby considered lighting a cigarette but decided against it

in case The Psychiatrist did suddenly appear. It would be one more thing to discuss. Ruby's total lack of regard for the well-being of her lungs. Truth of the matter was, Ruby liked her lungs fine, but she liked cigarettes even better. There had been valiant attempts to quit. Entire weeks spent putting in extra miles on her bicycle, gnawing a huge wad of Nicorette gum, breathing hard through her nose when the urges came. Eventually, some minor life detail would catch her off guard. The tension would build and, after a ten-minute moral struggle, Ruby would hightail it to the bodega at the corner of Surf and Stillwell to buy a pack of Marlboro Lights. She would barely make it out of the store before frantically ripping through the cellophane, extracting a cigarette, lighting up, and inhaling deeply, savoring the violation of her lungs. Afterward, Ed would smell the smoke on her and complain. *Why?* he'd ask, giving her that pained look. Ed liked Ruby's lungs too. In theory, Ed liked the entire five feet and four inches of Ruby Murphy, but it hadn't felt that way to her lately. Another thing to avoid telling The Psychiatrist. Providing Dr. Jody Ray ever showed up.

A whisper-thin young woman walked by, talking on a cell phone as her small white dog strained on its leash. The animal pulled its way right over to Ruby and began wagging its abbreviated tail, looking up at Ruby with limpid brown eyes. As Ruby bent down to pet the dog, the young woman yanked at the leash.

"It's okay. I love dogs," Ruby said.

The woman looked at Ruby blankly, said, "Hold on, Jerry,"

into her phone, then reached down, scooped the dog under her arm, and walked away, angry at her pet's forcing an unscheduled human interaction.

Ruby reflected that she'd like to have a dog. Instead, she had four cats. Furry sociopaths. It was slightly embarrassing. Even the pet food store people spoke to her gently, as if she weren't firing on all cylinders. It hadn't been Ruby's idea to have four cats. Two were hers; the other pair belonged to Ed. He had moved in a year earlier, mingling his few possessions with hers and adding his two cats to the tally. It was like a farm in their apartment. A farm above a Russian furniture store within spitting distance of the Cyclone roller coaster.

A cab suddenly veered to a stop a few feet in front of Ruby, its nose coming within inches of ramming a hydrant on the sidewalk. The back door was flung open and out came Dr. Jody Ray. She was all legs and white skirt suit. Her natural red hair caught the sun and held it.

"I'm so sorry, Ruby. There was terrible traffic," The Psychiatrist said.

"That's fine," Ruby drawled even though she'd rushed to make it there on time.

Ruby watched The Psychiatrist descend the three steps to the office door. Ruby felt mischievous and asked, "How are you?" Knowing full well that Dr. Jody Ray would deflect the question.

The Psychiatrist pivoted her head, looked Ruby in the eyes, and said: "Fine, thank you."

Ruby was delighted. For the first year of the doctor/patient relationship, Jody Ray had refused to answer direct questions and had invariably thrown questions back at Ruby in a clichéd way that stank three states away. The Psychiatrist still didn't volunteer many personal details, but she'd at least conceded to giving Ruby a ballpark figure of *fine* or *very well.* Even if it was a lie. Which, in this instance, it would prove to be.

As Ruby followed Jody Ray into the waiting room, she felt very tired. Ruby was no longer young. Well, to someone living in a retirement community she was. To herself, she was of moderate age. To the casting agent Ruby had once met with for three minutes (at the urging of an actor friend who'd been convinced that Ruby's slightly odd but intriguing looks could yield lucrative bit parts on television shows), Ruby had been very old. When Ruby admitted to being thirty-four, the casting agent made a horrified face that savaged fifty grand worth of plastic surgery, and, in a stage whisper, urged that Ruby never admit to this again.

"You're nineteen," the casting agent said. Ruby laughed. The casting agent never called, and Ruby continued in her downwardly mobile job at the Coney Island Museum. The job had gotten more interesting lately. Her boss, Bob, who ran both the sideshow and the museum, had decided to start a sideshow school. For a nominal fee, a civilian could learn to eat fire, drive nails up his nose, or walk on broken glass. The small but endless parade of applicants enlivened the atmosphere of the dusty little museum. There were worse fates than working there. And Ruby had experienced some of them. For example, one of her lovers had been murdered in front of her eighteen months earlier. Which was why Ruby first came to knock on Dr. Jody Ray's door. Ruby's life was not always easy, but it wasn't the sort of life where murder was commonplace. She would never get over it completely. She needed help.

The Psychiatrist was now standing in the middle of the waiting room, hunting for something in her yellow leather purse. Ruby let her eyes drift over the room. The walls were still a flat white. The loveseat was, as ever, covered in flower-motif brocade. To its right was a low table on top of which sat an immense fish tank, its inhabitants swimming and occasionally puckering their mouths. There were three office doors off the waiting area, but Ruby seldom saw the other psychiatrists whose names were engraved into a brass plaque on the front door. Ruby occasionally bumped into their patients in the waiting room and vigorously speculated about what might be wrong with them, but she almost never saw the other doctors.

The Psychiatrist seemed confused about which key opened her office door. As Ruby watched this uncharacteristic fumbling, she observed that Dr. Jody Ray's fingernails were chewed down. Ruby thought it was strange that she'd never noticed this before, stranger still that The Psychiatrist was a nail-biter. She was such a poised woman. Ruby was tempted to comment on the bitten nails. To ask exactly how a woman who evidently felt compelled to chew herself might be qualified to uncloud anyone's subconscious. Ruby stifled the urge.

The Psychiatrist at last fitted the correct key in the door and pushed it open. Ruby followed her in then flopped into an overstuffed armchair. She closed her eyes and listened to The Psychiatrist rustling as she settled herself. Familiar, soothing sounds. A depositing of the purse on the small bookcase under the window. The barely audible smoothing of the skirt. A shifting of weight as The Psychiatrist made herself comfortable.

Ruby waited ten or so seconds after the settling sounds had stopped. Then she waited longer. She enjoyed forcing The Psychiatrist to speak first.

"So," The Psychiatrist finally succumbed, "how was your week, Ruby?"

"Oh fine," Ruby said, wondering why she was lying. "How was yours?"

There was a tiny intake of breath followed by a startling response. "I've had better weeks, to be quite frank."

"Oh?" Ruby said, feeling a small thrill at the revelation.

"Yes. But please talk about yourself now." The Psychiatrist scowled at Ruby and, in that moment, looked old. Though the casting agent would have urged Jody Ray to claim herself barely thirty, The Psychiatrist, Ruby knew, was forty-five. Dr. Jody Ray took excellent care of herself. There was probably an exercise regime, vitamins, regular full-body exfoliation, and vigorous use of a drawer full of sex toys in addition to the appealingly dark and scruffy husband Ruby had met once. Ordinarily, Jody Ray looked to be in her mid-thirties. But just then, with a beam of afternoon sun snaking its way through the venetians, spotlighting a network of wrinkles around The Psychiatrist's eyes, Jody Ray looked old.

Ruby started feeling like a heel for playing games with The Psychiatrist. She launched into the first complaint.

"Ed is obsessed with that new horse I mentioned last session," Ruby offered. The Psychiatrist nodded slightly. She was used to hearing about Ruby's horse-trainer boyfriend's workaholism. How he lived and breathed horses. How he talked horses in his sleep. How he forgot to eat or bathe sometimes because his head was clouded with horses.

"He's spent two nights sleeping at the barn with the damn horse instead of coming home. I've been thrown over for a knock-kneed horse," Ruby said.

"Knock-kneed?" The Psychiatrist asked.

"Yes. Juan the Bullet is a knock-kneed New York breed. And he's tiny. He's a nice horse, but not that nice. Maybe Ed's obsessed with the horse because there's something missing between us."

Life had come into The Psychiatrist's eyes. She liked horses. It wasn't a girls-and-horses thing. Ruby found the whole girls-and-horses thing offensive and degrading to horses. No. As far as Ruby knew, The Psychiatrist did not walk around harboring erotic feelings for horses. The Psychiatrist's husband owned several racehorses trained by Ruby's friend Violet. It was Violet who'd introduced Ruby to The Psychiatrist after Ruby had watched Attila Johnson being murdered. Yes. Ruby's murdered lover had been named after a Hun. Ruby didn't remember how the original Attila had met his end, but her Attila had been shot by a sociopath. In front of her. After shooting Attila, the sociopath had left the scene of the crime. He had never threatened Ruby herself. He had left her there with her dead lover. There hadn't been a working phone in the place, and Ruby had stayed for hours, cradling Attila's lifeless head in her hands. Afterward, this image had haunted her. The blood from the small, neat bullet wound drying on her fingertips. The once vivid blue eyes paling as death did its work. Now, after sixteen months of visits to The Psychiatrist, the image was beginning to fade. The haunting would never stop, but the image was fading.

"All Ed thinks about is that damned horse," Ruby added after a pause.

"But it's probably not even about the horse," The Psychiatrist offered.

"Well then what?" Ruby asked. "He's sick of me, and the horse is an excuse?"

"Not sick of you. But avoiding something."

"Yeah. Me."

"Maybe you two need to talk."

Ruby shrugged. She felt something then. Something crawling down her neck. Maybe someone was walking on her grave. Maybe someone was talking about her. Maybe Ed was talking about her. Or thinking about her. One could only hope. The crawling went all the way down her spine and tucked itself into her tailbone. She suddenly needed to pee.

"I'm sorry, but I have to use the bathroom," Ruby said, feeling a slight thrill at this announcement. She'd never had to get up in the middle of a session before. This was new turf. Ruby loved new turf.

"By all means, please," The Psychiatrist said.

Ruby rose from her chair. As she pulled The Psychiatrist's office door closed behind her, her tailbone began to throb. She stood looking around at the small waiting room. The couch was in its place. The fish tank rested, as ever, on its low table. Ruby took a few steps toward the fish tank, suddenly feeling guilty over never having cared about the fish. Hailing from a family of borderline personalities who were indifferent at best to fellow humans but obsessively empathetic to creatures great and small, Ruby was supposed to care about fish. But she rarely looked at these or any fish. She made up for this now by staring into the tank. The fish were glorified goldfish. One was white with black spots, like a paint horse. The rest were orange. For some reason, they were all congregating at the bottom left corner of their tank, steering clear of a big *thing* that was taking up a good portion of real estate. Ruby wondered what the *thing* was. It was bluish white and, at its end, where it nubbed up against the bright green fish-tank pebbles, there was something that looked like toes.

Ruby's spine was on fire.

At the other end of the *thing*, the end sticking *out* of the tank, there was gore. Blood. Ruby blinked and took two steps closer. The fish were in very tight formation, squeezing next to one another as they tried to avoid contact with what appeared to be the lower half of a human leg. It occurred to Ruby that, in spite of the realness of the gore at the end of the leg, maybe this was a plastic leg. A prank by a disgruntled patient—maybe the chatty woman with flowing white hair who often emerged from her appointment with one of the other psychiatrists right when Ruby emerged from hers. Ruby mistrusted chatty people. Their chattiness was either a side effect of psychiatric medication that gave them verbal diarrhea or, alternatively, a sign of profound stupidity. To Ruby, excessive talking was one of the biggest offenses in the book. Right up there with pedophilia and bestiality. Maybe the chatty white-haired woman had snapped at having no one to chatter at and had put a plastic leg in the fish tank to make the world pay for its collective sin of not listening to her.

Ruby took one more step toward the leg. *This is no plastic leg,* Ruby thought. But it still didn't seem real.

Ruby reviewed her mental pictures of the previous half hour. She remembered glancing at the fish tank on the way into The Psychiatrist's office. There had not been a leg in the tank at that time.

Ruby noticed that the big toe of the foot was caught on some decorative coral. She started backing away and bumped up against a wall. She turned around and opened The Psychiatrist's door. The Psychiatrist smiled at Ruby expectantly.

"Jody," Ruby said, "something has gone wrong."

At first The Psychiatrist didn't move. She knitted her eyebrows and looked concerned. Ruby had to begin gesticulating wildly to get Jody up from her chair and into the waiting room.

Jody Ray's initial reaction seemed to be the same as Ruby's. She tilted her head slightly, looking at what she thought was a plastic leg. She started frowning at the bad joke. Ruby thought of things to say. Nothing seemed to fit the occasion.

As The Psychiatrist took a few steps closer to the fish tank, her jaw went slack. She stood gaping ahead for a few very long seconds; then her mouth started opening and closing. Just when Ruby thought Dr. Jody Ray was going to pass out, The Psychiatrist marched over to the fish tank, grabbed the leg, and pulled it out. Pinkness dripped onto the wood floor. The

Psychiatrist's already pale complexion went whiter than a snake's belly, and she dropped the leg.

"Oh shit," Jody said.

Another small victory for Ruby. The Psychiatrist had finally used profanity in front of her.

"Is it real?" Ruby asked even though she knew the answer.

"It's my husband's leg," the Psychiatrist said, casually indicating a birthmark on the side of the calf.

Ruby started wishing she were home, in bed, with the covers pulled over her head. Instead, she was standing there, watching her psychiatrist vomit. Dr. Jody Ray had evidently eaten Chinese food for lunch.

2. FIREBALL

Jody went into the bathroom to clean herself up, leaving Ruby to stare at the leg and the small pool of vomit near it. Ruby's body felt very heavy. She wanted to close her eyes and slump down to the floor. Instead, she started looking around the room, scanning for clues. Which is when she saw a piece of paper on the edge of the fish-tank table. Something was handwritten on the piece of paper: "No police. Just wait."

Again, Ruby felt like the whole thing was a bad joke. Who in his right mind would leave a note like that in the middle of a shared waiting room? What if someone else found it? The leg was real though. Presumably the note was too.

So the leg has been kidnapped, Ruby thought. No. That's wrong. The rest of the husband has been kidnapped. The leg is right here.

Ruby felt dizzy. She started riffling through the front pocket of her jeans, looking for a Fireball, which was the only thing other than a cigarette that would help her cope. Ruby kept Fireballs in her pockets for emergencies. This counted.

Ruby popped the bright red candy out of its wrapper and put it in her mouth. It had an odd, perfumy taste.

Ruby looked from leg to note to fish. She hoped the fish

hadn't been poisoned by leg viscera. She had a stab of self-doubt. This was a crisis, and she was thinking about her Fireball problem and the fish. *But people think strange things in a crisis,* she told herself. Self-involved things. It was only natural. Ruby had been standing on the Brooklyn Bridge when the World Trade Center towers had crumbled. Her first thought had been *I can't believe I'm actually getting to watch this happen firsthand.* Her first thought had been for her own horrible thrill. At least she admitted it. And anyway, the second thought had been for her friend Patty, who worked in one of the towers. Patty, though a little roughed up, survived.

Dr. Jody Ray emerged from the bathroom. Her face was skim-milk blue, and she looked twenty pounds thinner.

"I'm very sorry, Ruby," Jody said without looking Ruby in the eyes. "I'm sorry you've had to see this. But please go now."

"There's a note." Ruby motioned toward the note, which Jody immediately picked up.

"You probably shouldn't have touched that. Or the leg," Ruby said. Before becoming a workaholic horse-trainer, Ruby's boyfriend had been with the FBI. But it didn't take having an ex-Fed for a boyfriend to know you weren't supposed to touch evidence.

Jody Ray kept staring at the note, completely ignoring Ruby.

"Why don't you let me call the police?" Ruby said.

"No."

"Then I'll stay here while you call them."

"The police will not be called," The Psychiatrist said.

Ruby thought this was stupid.

"That's just stupid, Jody." She had never talked to her psychiatrist like this. She had cursed up a storm, ranted, and raved, but she'd never accused The Psychiatrist of being stupid for the simple reason that she wasn't. Until now. This was stupid. Ruby sucked her Fireball.

"Are you *eating* something?" The Psychiatrist asked, finally looking at Ruby.

"Fireball," Ruby shrugged. She'd talked about her Fireball problem in therapy. Had mentioned that even while putting in fifty miles on her bicycle, she sometimes sucked on a Fireball. She had tangentially speculated aloud as to whether Lance Armstrong, the Secretariat of bike riders, had ever had a Fireball. She preferred speculating about Lance Armstrong's possible familiarity with Fireballs to confiding what was inside her. The pit of dread she woke up with most mornings. The dread that didn't leave until she either got on her bike or went to take care of Jack, the retired racehorse she kept at a rundown stable in the worst neighborhood in Brooklyn.

"Can you *not* do that?" The Psychiatrist was staring at Ruby's mouth, genuinely offended that Ruby would suck on a piece of candy at a time like this.

"Sorry," Ruby said, removing the Fireball. She thought about the times Ed had asked her not to chew huge wads of gum. Ruby had trouble with moderation. She was fairly well adjusted, she had loved her late father, and she cherished her eccentric mother and difficult sister. She had had an alcohol problem and churned through a fair amount of love affairs, but who hadn't. On the whole, she was friends with herself. She just wasn't moderate.

Jody suddenly ducked back into the bathroom. Maybe another round of vomiting. Ruby stared at the half-sucked Fireball she was still holding in her hand. The red food-coloring coating was gone, and all that was left was a little white ball.

When Jody emerged, she was holding a garbage bag. Before Ruby could say anything, The Psychiatrist reached down, picked her husband's leg off the floor, and put it in the garbage bag. Ruby was glad she'd spit that Fireball out.

Ruby watched her psychiatrist tie a knot in the top of the garbage bag, walk into her office, and deposit the whole thing in a Carnegie Hall tote bag. Ruby didn't know what offended her most, the defilement of the Carnegie Hall tote bag or her psychiatrist's close-to-cavalier comportment.

Jody marched back out of her office and suddenly grabbed Ruby's elbow and unceremoniously guided her to the front door.

"Hey!" Ruby said as The Psychiatrist closed the door in her face.

Ruby stood there, blinking into the day. It was still bright under a cheerful, glaring orb of sun, but to Ruby it felt as though the temperature had plummeted. She shivered.

Ruby's first instinct was to call Ed even though Jody had ordered her not to involve him. She deliberated. Fished her phone out of her bright green backpack. As she stood holding the phone, it started vibrating in her hand. She flipped it open.

"Yeah?" She'd answered without checking the incoming number. Always dangerous.

"It's Ed." He sounded harried.

"Hi. You okay?" Ruby tried not to think of Jody or of the husband's leg.

"I'll be late," Ed said defensively.

"Of course," Ruby said.

"Don't be like that," he said.

"I'm not," Ruby lied. "I was going to cook something," she added. "I'll leave some in the fridge for you." Cooking *something* usually translated into Tofu Surprise. Cubes of tofu sautéed with vegetables and cayenne pepper. It wasn't bad. But it wasn't good either.

"Thanks," Ed said. "Everything okay?"

Ruby envisioned the leg.

"I'm just leaving Jody Ray's," she said.

"Oh." Ed never asked about her sessions. Ruby didn't know if this was due to a general distrust of psychiatry or to the fact that Ruby was seeing Jody in order to deal with the murder of an ex-lover.

"How's Juan the Bullet?" Ruby tried to sound cheerful, optimistic, anything but what she was.

"I think he's better," Ed said. "But I probably can't tell anymore. I'm worrying so much, objectivity's out the window. Never mind sanity."

"I know," Ruby said.

"I'm sorry," Ed said. "Sorry for how distracted I've been."

"It's fine," Ruby said. "Don't worry."

There was an amiable moment of silence. Then Ruby told Ed she was heading out to the barn to do her chores. In exchange for free board for Jack Valentine, the former racehorse who'd been given to her when a small fracture had ended his racing career, Ruby mucked out stalls, cleaned tack, and groomed the eight horses that lived in a ramshackle barn owned by her friend Coleman.

"I'll see you when you get home," Ruby said. "I'll wait up."

"That would be nice," Ed said softly.

Ruby flipped her phone shut. She half expected Ed to call back and ask her what was wrong. He didn't.

Ruby walked toward the signpost she'd chained her bike to. She preferred riding a bicycle through dense murderous traffic to taking the subway. She did have a car, but driving—which she'd just learned to do—terrified her. So she rode her bike. She sometimes felt like some sort of freak for riding a bicycle everywhere, but bike riding wasn't just the province of stoned messengers and people who worked in amusement park museums. In fact, thousands of New Yorkers did everything from ride all over the city in massive groups to race eight-thousand-dollar carbon-fiber bikes at the crack of dawn in Central Park. Though Ruby got her share of insults and angry drivers trying to kill her for sport, the bike was better than mass transit.

Ruby put two fingers in her pocket and found another Fireball. She popped it into her mouth then slowly pedaled east.

3. HELP

It was close to rush hour, the noise was dizzying, and the air hung thick over the buzzing traffic. A cab tried to kill Ruby, and she hated New York. Everyone who loved New York hated New York and fantasized about moving to Vermont. Some actually did move to Vermont. They pretended to be happy there, but Ruby knew they were secretly cold and bored. So she stayed in New York.

Ruby crossed through Queens to where it nudged up against the ass-end of Brooklyn. Planes flew low, homing in on nearby JFK Airport. Here and there, a seagull cut a path through the polluted sky.

On Linden Boulevard, Ruby rode up onto the sidewalk for a few blocks until she reached the side street that led down into the tiny neighborhood known as The Hole.

There had been a lot of rain lately, and most of it had gathered here, in this five-acre dent of land situated a few hundred yards from a long series of housing projects and highways. It was, as far as Ruby could tell, the strangest neighborhood in New York City. To one side was Howard Beach, a white working-class area jutted up against the periphery of unruly East New York. Squat in the middle of it all was a small area known as Lindenwood, where blue-collar home owners shared land with horses kept in ramshackle barns. The barns weren't entirely legal, but real estate there wasn't exactly valuable, so no one had done anything about it.

As Ruby got off to walk her bike through a patch of mud, she saw the woman she'd come to think of as Pee Lady, squatting between two parked cars. She was a fiftyish, reasonably well-dressed woman who, for whatever reason, chose to urinate in public places. This was the fourth time in a month that Ruby had seen her. As far as Ruby knew, Pee Lady had no business at The Hole. Ruby had never seen her near a horse or talking to anyone who kept a horse there, and she didn't seem to be friends with any of the home owners. No. The woman had wandered over from who-knows-where to pee there, between cars.

As Ruby walked by, Pee Lady looked up. Her pale eyes locked on Ruby's but nothing showed on her face. Ruby tried to think of something to say. Nothing came to mind.

The stable where Ruby's horse lived was a squat wooden building surrounded by a ten-foot-tall chain-link fence. Some days, Coleman, the stable owner, left his two pit bulls, Honey and Pokey, to guard the place. The dogs weren't there now though. Coleman had probably taken them for a romp along Jamaica Bay, or to the posh doggie bakery in nearby Queens where the pits salivated over treats and stared down the designer dogs owned by the wealthy matrons who made up the bulk of the bakery's patronage.

Ruby unlocked the gate, wheeled her bike in, and leaned it against the fence. She walked into the small dark barn. As her eyes adjusted to the dimness, she involuntarily pictured

Jody's husband's leg in the Carnegie Hall tote. She could still see the chunks of gore at the end of the leg. She took a deep breath and shook herself off the way a dog would after a nap.

Ruby's horse recognized her footsteps and whinnied intensely. As Ruby came closer, the big bay gelding shook his head and lifted his upper lip, exposing enormous yellow teeth. This was his way of asking for a peppermint. He wouldn't let Ruby do anything with him until she'd produced the requisite piece of pink and white striped candy, a thing he'd gotten a taste for at the track.

"Yeah yeah," Ruby said. She took off her backpack and dug around until she found a small plastic bag full of peppermints. She usually kept a stash in her trunk in the tack room but had run out. She'd had the nerve to come empty-handed a few days in a row but now, finally, had the goods. The horse kept shaking his head as Ruby unwrapped a piece of candy.

"Here." She held out her palm, candy in the middle, and the big gelding greedily took it. As he noisily rolled the mint around in his mouth, Ruby got her cell phone out and dialed Jody's office number. She wasn't sure exactly what she might say to her psychiatrist. But she felt compelled to call.

The machine came on: "You've reached the office of Jody Ray. Please leave a message after the tone." Ruby hung up. She took a deep breath and closed her eyes. The horse was still clacking the mint against his teeth. Ruby desperately wanted to call Jane. Ruby had been friends with Jane for close to twenty years, and no one knew Ruby better. But Jane was off in India for the summer, studying yoga and Sanskrit, living in a shack without running water or electricity. She'd been gone two weeks and wouldn't be back for another month. Ruby couldn't imagine what kind of shape she'd be in then. At this rate, she'd explode within forty-eight hours. First, though, there were barn chores to do. Eight stalls to be mucked, eight horses to be groomed. It was monotonous and grueling. Exactly what she needed.

Ruby wasn't sure how much time had passed when her ass started vibrating. She'd tucked her phone into her back pocket but had forgotten to switch it from Vibrate to Ring.

"Yeah?" She pulled the phone out, flipping it open without checking the incoming number.

"Ruby, this is Jody."

"Hi," Ruby said. She felt idiotic saying *hi* under the circumstances, but what else was she going to say?

"Where are you?" Jody asked.

"At the barn, doing chores. What's happening?" *What's happening* sounded even more stupid.

"Nothing good, I can tell you that much."

"What can I do?"

"Nothing. That's why I'm calling. To reiterate what I said earlier. Please don't tell Ed about any of this. Please don't tell anyone. My husband's life is at stake."

"It is? Has he been kidnapped?"

"I cannot discuss any of this with you. And I have to apologize once more for what I've put you through. I never intended any such thing."

"It's fine," Ruby said, even though it wasn't.

"Good-bye," Jody said, suddenly hanging up in Ruby's ear.

Ruby hated being hung up on. She was fairly certain that

one of the things most wrong with modern society was rudeness. Hanging up in someone's ear was inexcusable.

Ruby immediately tried to call Jody back, but the call went straight to voice mail. She flipped her phone shut and put it back in her pants pocket. She stared at the pitchfork she was holding and fleetingly imagined impaling herself through the prefrontal cortex with it. Fascination with brain injuries had almost led Ruby to apply to medical school in her late twenties. But not quite. She was not good at taking tests or memorizing things. So she'd continued on her path as a drifter. And now was shoveling horse shit in exchange for free board for a recovering racehorse she'd never ridden. Ruby was deathly afraid of actually riding her horse. She just kept him as a pet. And worked many hours a week for the privilege of doing so.

The pet in question was out back in the paddock now, and he whinnied, as if sensing he'd been thought of. Ruby put the pitchfork down, walked out of the barn, and went to look at her horse. Jack was standing in the center of the paddock, head high, ears pointed forward. He was looking at something, though Ruby had no idea what. After a few seconds, he lost interest in whatever it was and trotted over to where Ruby was standing. He skidded to a halt cartoon-style, stared at Ruby as if he'd never seen her before in his life, then relaxed, stuck his muzzle out toward her, and carefully nuzzled at her left ear.

Ruby was completely absorbed in wondering if Jack was going to bite her ear, and she didn't hear Triple Harrison coming up behind her.

"Morning, sunshine," he said, startling Ruby.

She flipped around.

"Oh. Triple, hi."

"Skittish today are we?"

"I didn't hear you come up behind me. You shouldn't do that."

"Sorry, doll," he shrugged and tried to look handsome.

Triple Harrison was a likable drifter who lived in a mold-eaten house across from Coleman's barn. Like Ruby, he owned a former racehorse. A bay mare named Kiss the Culprit who'd actually won a few in her day but was now fat, lazy, and unspeakably happy to be Triple's pet.

"How are you?" Ruby asked, knowing it was a loaded question. Triple never gave the expected answer of *Fine*. He liked to report, in detail, exactly how he was. Usually, this involved some sort of drama at his job. He worked as a lifeguard at a swank health club all the way over in Park Slope. For some reason, he couldn't simply mind his business and make sure no one drowned. He was endlessly tying to befriend the swimmers and, now and then, dating a female swimmer. It invariably ended badly, and Ruby had to hear all about it. Lately, it had occurred to her that Triple told her all these grisly details to invoke pity so that maybe she'd sleep with him. She wouldn't and had told him as much a few times over, but he never listened.

"I'm fine," Triple said, uncharacteristically.

Obviously, something was wrong. "What's the matter?" Ruby asked.

"I'm low."

"Why?" Ruby asked.

"I'm just low." He said in a small voice, "Can I have a hug?"

Ruby rolled her eyes. "Yeah, I guess."

Triple was a hugger. You wouldn't expect it to look at him. He was tall with gangly limbs he'd never grown into even though he was at least thirty-five. His arms were covered in faded jailhouse tattoos, and his hair was shaggy. Ruby was sure his toenails were jagged and that he liked women who threw plates at him as a prelude to sex.

Ruby let him hug her for a few seconds then took a step back.

"Where's that boyfriend of yours?" Triple was looking Ruby over head to toe.

She shrugged. "He got a really good two-year-old to train. It's consuming him."

"I'm all for being consumed by a horse, but it don't mean I wouldn't be keeping an eye on my girl," he said, his grin growing to shit-eating proportions.

"Shut up, Triple," Ruby said. For three seconds, she toyed with the idea of telling Triple about the leg. After four seconds, she realized this was an incredibly bad idea.

"Always a pleasure chatting with you, but I've got work to finish in the barn," Ruby said.

"Want some help?" Triple asked.

"I'm almost done, it's okay. But thanks." Ruby said. She opened the gate to the paddock and snapped a lead rope onto Jack's halter. She wanted to get her horse back in the barn before Triple started in on his favorite refrain.

"When you gonna ride that hoss?"

Too late.

"Soon," Ruby said. She was tired of people asking when she was going to ride the damn horse, for the simple fact was that she had no idea when she was going to ride the damned horse. She was terrified at the prospect. She had first been around horses in her early twenties when she'd worked as a groom for two years outside Tampa, Florida. She'd learned how to ride but would never be a very confident rider. The idea of getting on a Thoroughbred who didn't know how to do anything other than gallop around a racetrack wasn't exactly compelling. She was putting it off.

"How soon?" Triple persisted.

Ruby looked right at him. There were tiny snakes of red in the whites of his eyes. He had a pimple on his forehead. "Soon," she repeated.

"Okay, okay." Triple put his palms out in a defensive gesture. "No need to get angry."

"I'm not," Ruby lied. She was. At herself. Hated her own chicken-shittedness. Usually, she didn't see herself as a chicken, but then things like this came up. Things that were evidence of cowardice. It was awful.

As Ruby led Jack toward the barn, Triple wished Ruby a nice day. She grunted without turning around.

Once she'd finished her chores, Ruby spent a pleasant half hour grooming her horse. He was an agreeable, friendly horse. His niceness, his very horsiness, soothed Ruby. Almost enough to take away the image of the severed leg. Almost.

It was dark by the time Ruby wheeled her bike out of the stable yard and locked the gate. She stood staring at the little barn as she tried to remember if she'd forgotten anything. She hadn't fed the barn cat, but he hadn't been around and probably had gorged on mouse corpses and passed out on a bale of hay somewhere.

Ruby got onto her bike and started pedaling. Her leg muscles had stiffened during the time she'd been at the barn, and the first few revolutions of the wheels were painful. She was riding up the incline to Linden Boulevard, cursing her legs for aching, when she felt a car behind her. At the top of the incline, she put one foot to the ground and turned around to see whose car it was. She was expecting Triple. Maybe playing at following her home. Mock stalking the way he liked to. But it was just some random blue car with a random dark-haired man at the wheel. There was something vaguely familiar about the man's broad face, but he didn't show any signs of recognizing her so Ruby got back on the bike and pedaled away.

Night was coming on like heartache.

4. HEIGHTS

Ruby rode home to Coney Island the back way, avoiding the madness of Surf Avenue. Its chaos was one of the things Ruby loved most about Coney, but not tonight, not at the end of a day that had featured a severed leg in a fish tank. No. Tonight Ruby needed quiet backstreets.

She rode up onto the sidewalk in front of her building and got off the bike. Her lungs were sore and her ass hurt slightly. She liked that. She liked the various pains and indignities she inflicted on her body. Helped keep her mind quiet.

As she fished her house keys from her backpack, Ruby looked up at the recently renovated Stillwell Avenue subway station. She did this almost every day but never got used to it. Not that it was bad-looking. Just slightly futuristic, almost German, and at odds with the decaying community it served. Coney had been declining for a long long time, and for just as long there had been rumors of casinos and Disney and Donald Trump. Now though, it seemed that something major was truly on the verge of happening. Something that very possibly would destroy Ruby's home. Either literally, if the building she rented in was sold, or figuratively, if Astroland were razed and Mickey Mouse put in its place.

Ruby hoisted her bike onto her shoulder and climbed the

uneven stairs to the second floor. She glanced toward her lone neighbors' door. Pietro Ramirez and his wife, Elsie, usually left it open, especially in summer when the top floor of the old two-story building was a sauna. Not tonight though. Ruby wasn't sure if she was relieved over the avoided social contact or not. She liked her neighbors, was sometimes even grateful for Elsie's borderline busybody-ness that forced Ruby to confess whatever was on her mind. Tonight it would have been awkward. Intuitive Elsie would have prodded and been hurt when Ruby failed to come clean with the details.

Ruby unlocked her apartment door, put her bike against the wall, and nearly tripped when Stinky, her enormous black and white cat, launched himself at her calves.

Ruby sat down on the floor, scooped the cat into her arms, and squeezed him. The rest of the cat pack came to stare at her, politely willing her to prepare their dinner as they likely counted their blessings that the human wasn't trying to squeeze them too.

Once she felt vaguely restored to sanity through the grace of her fat cat, Ruby got up and went into the kitchen. She flicked the light switch but nothing happened. Ed had forgotten to replace the bulb. Ruby was too short to reach it, and climbing up on the table to do it would make her weak-kneed since she'd developed a fear of heights after turning thirty.

She fed the cats in the dark, banging her shin into a table leg in the process. Another pain to catalog next to the sore lungs and stinging ass.

As the cats made their savage meat-eating sounds, Ruby retrieved her phone from her backpack and flipped it open to make sure Jody hadn't called. She hadn't. There were several thousand things Ruby needed to do, but she was suddenly bone tired. She dropped down onto the couch and lay on her back. She reached over to the coffee table for the book she was nursing that week. *Rats: Observations on the History and Habitat of the City's Most Unwanted Inhabitants* was a splendidly entertaining tome, but Ruby nodded off after two pages.

———

RUBY WATCHED in horror as an enormous rat crawled up her leg. She felt a hand on her shoulder and heard a voice in her ear.

"Ruby, hey, Ruby."

She opened her eyes. Ed was peering at her as if she was a medical curiosity.

"Hi," she said.

"You were screaming."

"I was having a nightmare." Before nodding off, Ruby had gotten to a passage about rats getting onto crowded subway cars and riding to the next stop. This notion had successfully distracted her from the image of Jody's husband's leg, and she'd fallen asleep. Dreaming of rats.

Ruby scooted her body back on the couch, making room for Ed as she told him about the dream rat crawling up her leg.

"Why are you reading about rodents?"

"It's fascinating."

"Rats?"

"Very primal."

Ed smiled and shook his head. He looked exhausted.

There were crevices around his mouth, valleys beneath his eyes. His glasses were filthy. His hair needed cutting. Still, Ruby liked looking at him. This was one of the things that made her think she was in it for the long haul with Ed. She always found him beautiful. Even when he wasn't.

"Is Juan okay?" Ruby dug her fingers into Ed's forearm, kneading the tight narrow muscles there.

"I think so. He's eating good, not acting like anything's bothering him." Ed looked worried while saying it. He hadn't convinced himself that his prized little horse was truly all right.

"I didn't make dinner," Ruby announced.

Ed was relieved but tried not to show it.

"We'll go out."

"It's late." Ruby had just looked at the little clock atop the TV. It was nearly ten.

"Brighton Diner?" Ed asked.

"Okay."

The place was loud, the food was lousy, and the waitresses were hostile. But Ruby didn't mind. Just as she enjoyed brutalizing her body, Ruby liked stoically weathering waitresses' minor abuses, figuring she was getting her quota of pain from the universe for the week and could ward off anything worse happening.

It was after eleven by the time Ruby and Ed walked back from the diner, both a little queasy and sleepy from greasy omelettes.

Astroland was still thriving. Girls in tight jeans and belly-baring tops. Hipster white kids looking nervous at being vastly outnumbered by dark-skinned folks. Here and there, an old Russian couple, disgusted at what the world was coming to.

Ruby fell asleep spooning behind Ed, marveling that they'd gotten through the evening without her telling him what had happened that day. It almost seemed like any other night. Almost.

5. MAGIC

At three-thirty in the morning, Ed got up and went into the kitchen to poach four eggs. It was Wednesday, one of Ruby's days off from the museum, the day when she usually accompanied Ed to the track, spending a few hours at Belmont before going to The Hole. Today though, her body was protesting the lack of sleep. Her eyes wouldn't open and her legs were stiff. She slowly got out of bed and started stretching. She hated imagining what getting older would be like. At this rate, she'd need a full body cast by age fifty.

Ruby went into the kitchen and fed the cats and ate her poached eggs while Ed showered. He was ready long before she was and waited at the door, drumming his fingers on the door frame.

"I'm sorry I'm slow—don't be impatient," Ruby said.

"I'm not impatient."

Ruby kept feeling as if she was forgetting something, but she couldn't figure out what. Maybe it was just the secret she was keeping from Ed. Maybe the secret was disorienting her. She followed Ed into the hall and locked up.

Ramirez, who probably hadn't been to bed yet, had his door open. He was standing in the middle of his yellow kitchen, looking put out about something. He'd gotten paunchy lately, evidently having sympathetic swelling with his pregnant wife. Though he'd outdone her by now. Where the diminutive Elsie still barely showed at six months, Ramirez looked ready to birth a basketball.

"Morning," said Ruby.

"Morning," Ramirez said, barely more than a grunt. He nodded at Ed then turned his back and started fiddling with the stove.

Ruby and Ed walked to the lot where Ed kept his twenty-year-old red Ford pickup and Ruby kept the 1974 Mustang she never drove. Ruby climbed in the passenger side and pulled the squeaking seat belt around her waist.

The sun hadn't dreamed of coming up yet.

———

ED WAS LOST in thought, and Ruby spent most of the ride over to Belmont dwelling on Jody's husband's leg. She tried to think of other things. Food. Sex. Bicycles. Space and Time. World Travel. Cholera. But she kept seeing it. In the fish tank. On the floor. Unceremoniously tucked into Jody's Carnegie Hall tote.

The moment Ed drove in through the main stable gate though, the magic happened: Ruby absorbed the sight of horse buildings, horse people, and horses, horses, horses as far as the eye could see. A sea of horses. And all was better.

Ed parked the truck at the end of the shed row he shared with Blake Reta, a successful trainer who had a small army of grooms and assistants working for him. All Ed could afford was Nicky, a part-time groom who was always late. And Nicky was definitely late this morning. Ed's horses hadn't been fed, and every last one was standing stoically still and looking more than a little wounded. Ed barely glanced at them though. He made a beeline for Juan the Bullet's stall and immediately knelt by the colt's bandaged leg.

Ruby stared at the horse and the horse stared back. He wasn't much to look at. A dullish light chestnut, barely fifteen hands. Where other two-year-olds were already rippled with muscle, Juan looked like somebody's backyard horse. But Ruby had to admit he had a good face. A thick white blaze started under his forelock and ended in a blur near his nose. The oversized nostrils were a little ungainly looking, but some people theorized that big nostrils meant a horse could take in more air—and run faster. What really distinguished Juan the Bullet were his eyes. He had beautiful, intelligent eyes. Most of the good ones did. And this is what made Ruby think that just maybe her boyfriend's lunacy was justified. That this funny-looking little horse might do some running at some point.

Satisfied that the horse's leg hadn't fallen off during the night, Ed stood up and came out of the stall.

"Help me feed?" he asked Ruby.

"Sure," she said. She liked being put to work. For a few minutes anyway.

By the time Nicky finally showed up, Ed had Ruby mucking out stalls. Nicky stuck his head into the stall where Ruby was working and flashed his gap-toothed smile. Ruby gruffly handed him her pitchfork.

"Thanks," Nicky said brightly. No apology, just that smile.

Ruby had her doubts about Nicky. He was a nice-looking man in his early thirties. He was well spoken, had all his teeth, and didn't seem to fit the profile of the kind of guy who suddenly got frustrated with his dull little life and gave it all up to go rub racehorses. Ed had never seen a reason to probe Nicky about his intentions or origins though, so Ruby left it alone.

"Nicky took over," she told Ed, finding her boyfriend back in Juan the Bullet's stall.

"Good," Ed said, even though Ruby suspected he liked watching her muck out stalls.

"I'm going over to see Violet," she said.

"You coming back?"

"Probably not. It's getting late. It'll take me a while still to get over to The Hole." Ruby would call a cab after she'd visited with Violet.

"Why can't you just drive that car of yours?" Ed asked.

"Don't want to." Ruby had gotten around by bicycle for so long that she had trouble seeing cars as anything other than evil machines out to kill her. She knew this was unreasonable, but she didn't really care.

"Okay." Ed surrendered. He leaned over to kiss Ruby good-bye. "You okay?" he asked as he pulled back.

"Yeah, why?"

"You seem funny."

"Funny?" Ruby tried to look innocent, like she'd never seen a severed leg in her life.

"Never mind." Ed said, "Call me later?"

"I will."

———

VIOLET'S OFFICE DOOR was wide open so Ruby walked right in. And nearly choked when she found Jody Ray there, sitting on Violet's dirty couch. Ruby blinked.

"Oh, Ruby," Jody said listlessly.

The Psychiatrist was wearing a knee-length lemon-colored dress made of translucent material. She was holding a large yellow purse. She was paler than ever, and her bright hair had dulled. She looked as if she'd been up doing coke all night.

"I was looking for Violet," Ruby said.

"Yes, she's around." Jody waved her hand. She seemed small even though she wasn't.

"I guess I'll wait for her," Ruby said.

"Oh. Yes," Jody said weakly. This was probably the last thing she wanted. But she didn't have the strength to protest. She busied herself digging through her purse.

Outside the office, there was the sound of hooves against dirt as a hotwalker guided a horse past the door.

"I've been asked to come up with money," Jody said after a thick three-minute silence.

"A lot?" Ruby tried to seem casual, as though she'd fully expected Jody to start talking.

"Of course."

"I'm sorry. And you still haven't called anyone?"

"No," Jody said without moving her lips.

"You're endangering your husband. If he's even alive." Ruby was surprised she'd actually said it aloud.

Jody finally looked Ruby in the eyes. "I've been through this before," she said.

"Your husband's been kidnapped before?"

"No. Me."

"You were kidnapped?" Ruby was incredulous.

"When I was younger. My parents did as the kidnappers asked, and I was returned unharmed."

Ruby instinctively knew further revelations were forthcoming.

"What did your parents do for a living?" Ruby asked. It wasn't what she'd meant to ask. It had just popped out.

"They were psychiatrists," Jody answered as if it were a natural question.

"Both?"

Jody nodded.

"Oh," said Ruby. No wonder the woman chewed her fingernails. "So you're planning on coming up with the money?"

"That's why I'm here. I have seventy-two hours to get it, but I don't have many resources. There was a substantial offer made some weeks ago for one of Tobias's horses, and I'm here to see if Violet can sell the horse and collect the money in such a short time. Violet doesn't know why I need the money so quickly, and I'd like to keep it that way." Jody was staring at Ruby but she didn't really seem to see her. Her blue eyes were bloodshot.

Ruby struggled for something to say. Then was saved by Violet coming through the office door.

"Oh!" Violet said, "Ruby!"

Violet looked drawn. This was hardly a shock. Jody's husband's colt, Fearless Jones, was hands down the most exciting horse Violet and Henry had trained in years. Ruby knew it had to be a heartbreak. She wished she could tell Violet that Jody had an extraordinarily valid reason for doing something this rash.

Ruby stood up to hug Violet.

"You might not want to do that." Violet pulled back. "Our shower is broken. I'm afraid I'm quite ripe."

"You smell fine to me," Ruby said, realizing this sounded peculiar. No one seemed to notice though.

"Violet, you're very kind to help me," Jody said, rising from the couch and smoothing her dress down over her thighs.

Violet nodded. She looked as if she was about to cry.

"Could I have a word with you, Ruby?" Jody asked.

"Oh," Ruby said, surprised, "sure." She looked at Violet.

"I have an awful lot to do, Ruby," Violet said weakly. "We'd better have coffee another time."

"Okay." Ruby felt overwhelmingly useless for not being able to console her friend.

On her way out, Ruby touched Violet's shoulder. Violet tried to smile.

Ruby followed Jody Ray over to the dirt road behind the barn, where Jody stopped walking and turned to Ruby.

"I'm sorry for this," she said, looking past Ruby.

"For what?"

"For what you've seen in the last twenty-four hours. For what it must be putting you through."

"It's not putting me through anything. Though it is frustrating. And horrible for poor Violet."

"Yes," Jody said, "poor Violet."

Suddenly, Jody's face folded in on itself, and she started crying. "I'm sorry," she said, wiping tears from the corners of her eyes.

Her mascara had streaked a little.

"You have streaks," Ruby said, touching under her own eyes.

"Thank you." Jody dabbed at her eyes, gulped air in, then started crying again.

To her own amazement, Ruby draped an arm around her psychiatrist's shoulders. She felt Jody stiffen. She considered removing her arm but didn't. Instead, she started talking. Reiterating that Jody should call the cops. Jody didn't move or say anything. After a while, Ruby removed her arm. She felt like an idiot.

"I know what I'm about to ask is probably wrong," Jody said, "but I desperately need help." She pushed a long strand of hair off her forehead.

"Okay," Ruby said tentatively.

"Would you consider coming with me to Tobias's apartment to look through his things? I haven't been able to bring myself to do it."

Ruby frowned, confused.

Jody clarified: "We've been separated for a while. He has a studio apartment in the East Fifties."

"Oh," Ruby said. It was getting really weird. But of course Ruby liked that. "I guess so," she said.

Jody was still staring right through Ruby and didn't seem to have heard her.

"So do you want to go now?" Ruby asked.

"Oh," Jody snapped out of it, "yes."

"How long will it take?"

"Take? I don't know."

"An hour? Two?"

"I don't know." Jody seemed frustrated. "I guess this is a bad idea."

"No," Ruby protested, "I was just wondering how long it would take. I have to go tend to my horse."

"Oh, the horse, right," Jody said. "Yes. Well, two hours tops."

Ruby had never heard Jody say anything as colloquial as *tops*.

"All right, that's fine," Ruby said.

Jody was staring off into the distance. At what, Ruby didn't know.

"Should we go then?" Ruby prodded her.

"Oh," Jody's eyes focused, "yes, let's."

She turned and started walking very quickly toward the parking lot. Ruby, who was a few inches shorter, had to trot to keep up with her.

Jody's car was an exquisite cream-colored Mercedes sedan from the 1980s. Ruby got in the passenger side, settling into the red leather seat. Jody slammed her door shut and kicked off her shoes.

"I like to feel the pedals," she said.

This struck Ruby as an overly intimate revelation—that Jody's liking to feel the car's acceleration shooting up through her feet somehow meant she was sexually voracious, which wasn't something Ruby really wanted to think about. Speculating about other people's sex lives was sometimes entertaining, but when that person was your psychiatrist, the whole thing took on unpleasant overtones.

"Oh" was all Ruby said.

Jody focused on driving, and Ruby was left to her own thoughts. She felt particularly alive at the prospect of helping her psychiatrist look through her husband's things. She had actively decided to do something unusual and that was making her tingle. Ruby had always been slightly purposeless. She liked life, but she'd let it shove her wherever it wanted and she never pushed back.

"Are you okay?" Jody asked after a ten-minute silence.

Ruby was startled.

"I'm feeling mediocre," she heard herself say. Yet another thing popping out uncensored. She glanced over at Jody. The Psychiatrist was frowning.

"What do you mean by that?"

"You know. How I do so many things but don't excel at any of them." The woman was her shrink, after all.

"What brought this on?"

"I'm not sure."

"I was under the impression you excelled at many things."

"At what?" Ruby asked, "I don't have a stressful but stimulating job the way most New Yorkers do. I don't train racehorses or even do something noble like teach yoga to mental defectives the way my best friend does."

"You're not supposed to say 'mental defectives.'"

"Half the crazy people I know would refer to themselves that way."

"What about the other half?"

"I wouldn't use the phrase in front of them."

Jody arched an eyebrow.

"My husband is a mental defective."

"What?"

"He was my patient. Initially a suicide attempt."

"The husband whose leg was . . . ?"

"Only one I've got."

Ruby stared at The Psychiatrist.

"You're going to need years of therapy just to get over having been a patient of mine," Jody said then. She let out a small laugh. Ruby didn't laugh back.

"Does your husband's condition have anything to do with his having been kidnapped?"

"Not that I'm aware of."

"You have to call the authorities, Jody."

"Don't start with that again. I have a plan."

"This is crazy."

"I'll grant you that. And I'd like to reiterate that you don't have to do this, Ruby. I never intended to involve you in any way."

"It's fine."

"You're a kind and lovely woman."

"That and two bucks will get me on the subway. But thank you. I appreciate the sentiment."

"Don't be flip."

"I'm not."

They fell silent.

The traffic wasn't too bad, and Jody had to circle Tobias's block only three times to find a parking spot.

Tobias's street was a pleasant, mostly residential block. There were nice brownstones. A dry cleaner. People walking designer dogs.

The building was a three-story brownstone that had been sectioned off into small apartments. The husband's apartment was on the second floor in the back. As Jody fumbled with the keys, Ruby stared at her psychiatrist's chewed-down fingernails. She understood their provenance now: psychiatrist parents and a mental defective husband.

After getting the door open, Jody hesitated. Ruby stood behind her, waiting. She was on the verge of saying something when Jody walked forward.

The apartment was a large, L-shaped studio with two floor-to-ceiling windows looking out over a dense green garden. A massive sleigh bed was pushed against one wall, a desk and computer against another. A TV roosted on a stand near the bed. There was no sofa.

Jody walked over to the desk, sat down, and touched the computer keyboard. The screen woke up, and Ruby saw that the desktop pattern was a win photo of a racehorse.

Ruby came closer and stood looking over The Psychiatrist's shoulder as Jody opened the husband's e-mail program. Ruby and Ed shared a computer, but Ruby didn't think she'd ever be able to breach his privacy and read his e-mail. Even if Ed's leg had been cut off.

Jody suddenly got up and walked away from the computer. "I can't go through his mail like this. Would you do it?" Her face was pinched.

"What should I look for?"

"I don't know," Jody shrugged, "anything suspicious."

Ruby had no idea what might be construed as suspicious, but she sat down anyway and started reading through the man's saved mail. There was some correspondence between Tobias and a woman named Bess who he seemed to play Scrabble with frequently. There were several notes from Violet detailing billing for the three horses she trained for Tobias. Nothing of consequence.

Ruby started looking through the outgoing mail and found something more interesting. Right there for anyone to see. Or at least anyone who happened to go through his e-mail. Ruby felt her stomach tighten.

6. UNFIT

The note was addressed to Elvin.Miller@gmail.com, but there wasn't any salutation in the e-mail itself: "She will be in her office at that time. You can call her there. It will all go smoothly."

It could have been a note about almost anything, but Ruby knew this was it. She glanced over at her psychiatrist, who was on her hands and knees, looking through a shoebox in the closet. *It will all go smoothly.* Had Tobias had himself kidnapped? And who would be idiot enough to arrange that kind of thing and then leave evidence of it on his computer? It didn't make any sense.

"Jody?"

Jody was startled and dropped something. A pair of scissors. Why was she holding a pair of scissors? Ruby had a brief image of her psychiatrist stabbing her with the scissors. Then she thought tangentially of Edward Scissorhands and, for the thousandth time, wished he actually existed. She got like that sometimes. Insanely whimsical. A girl had to get through the day.

The Psychiatrist arched an eyebrow at Ruby.

"You should see this," Ruby said.

Jody got up, smoothed her dress over her legs, and came to look over Ruby's shoulder. She was still holding the scissors.

"Oh," Jody said after reading the note a few times.

"Did he have himself kidnapped?" Ruby asked.

"Evidently, yes."

"Really?"

"Yes, very possibly," Jody said in a weak voice.

"And had a leg cut off?"

"It seems rash. But Tobias can be rash. He's been known to do very sick things." Jody was completely cavalier, as though loss of limb and kidnapping were commonplace occurrences in her life.

"Why on earth would your husband have himself kidnapped?"

"Because he knew I'd pay. Without asking questions or involving the authorities. And then he would keep the money. He has none."

"I thought he was well off." Ruby remembered Violet telling her about Tobias's small fortune.

"He lost most of it. He gambles, of course. And buys bad stocks. What little is left I control. I had him declared unfit."

"Oh." Ruby thought about the Fireball in her front pocket. She knew this wasn't the time or the place for it. Which made her want it all the more. "Couldn't he just ask you for some money?"

"He could. But wouldn't. A fierce and bordering-on-perverse pride," Jody said, staring out the tall window. "What I don't understand is his failure to think this through in the slightest," she added.

Ruby waited. She stared at the greenery outside the windows. She imagined jumping out the window, stripping off all her clothing, running naked through the garden. She thought of the Brooklyn Botanic Garden and how she had run naked there on a dare as a teenager. It had felt delicious and raw. Why she was having a sudden urge to run through a garden naked right now, she didn't know.

"The only valuable thing Tobias has left is the colt. Fearless Jones." Jody continued, "And he knows I'll have to sell the horse to get the money." Jody walked over to the bed and sat down very slowly, as though she suddenly weighed hundreds of pounds. She smoothed her dress across her lap. Ruby wondered if the dress-smoothing was a nervous tic. The way Lance Armstrong pulled at the seams of his bike shorts during particularly taxing moments in a race.

"But this is all just a prank," Ruby said. "You're not actually going to sell the horse, are you? You'll find Tobias and talk him down."

"Two can play this game," said Jody. "And anyway, we still don't know," she added. "This may not be what it seems." She motioned at the computer screen. "There is a chance he has genuinely been kidnapped."

Sun was pouring in through the tall windows, shining right into Ruby's eyes. She got up from the chair, realized there wasn't anywhere else to sit, then unceremoniously lay down on the floor and closed her eyes.

"What are you doing?"

"Waiting for it all to go away," Ruby said.

"Which brings me to my point."

"What point?" Ruby asked, eyes still closed.

"I've fucked up again."

"How so?"

"I shouldn't have brought you here."

"Don't tell me, I should go now?" Ruby asked, keeping her eyes glued shut.

"Right."

"You're not serious?"

"Very."

Ruby had finally had enough. She got up off the floor, walked to the door, and didn't look back. Ruby half expected Jody to call out after her, but she didn't.

Ruby was fuming. She hated being jerked around. In the past, if a boyfriend had exhibited the slightest trace of jerking behavior, she'd left without a second thought. Women friends were supposed to be above that kind of thing, and one's psychiatrist *really* didn't have any business pulling that kind of stunt. But, as Ruby was discovering, her psychiatrist was no ordinary psychiatrist. Nor an ordinary woman. No. Jody Ray didn't have an ordinary bone in her body. Which didn't make Ruby any less furious about the jerking.

Ruby had a moment of disorientation when she reached the street. The day was too bright, the kind to make people feel guilty for even a slightly dark thought. And Ruby was having thousands of dark thoughts.

Heading for the subway, Ruby passed Jody's cream-colored Mercedes. She had an urge to kick it.

Ruby caught the 6 train to the L, riding it nearly the entire length of Brooklyn before switching at Broadway Junction for the A train. On the A there was a gaggle of kids, not more than thirteen years old but loud and completely foul-mouthed. *Motherfucker* this, *suck my dick* that, *I'm gonna fuck you up the ass,* etc. Ruby and the few other passengers on the car stared down at their laps. Ruby had been a wild kid. She'd run with a pack who vandalized phone booths and jumped the train-yard fences to graffiti the trains. She'd even had her own tag: Fatal Pop. She'd been wild, irreverent, but never rude to individuals. Even at the height of teen angst she'd hated rudeness.

At Grant Avenue, Ruby emerged from the subway, crossed North Conduit, and walked over to Linden Boulevard. The day was even brighter here where the buildings were low and the trees never grew enough to afford much shade. Ruby passed the incongruous flower shop that occupied space near a muffler shop and a gas station. The flower shop owner, a fifty-ish white woman with a very tan hide, nodded at Ruby. For no reason other than Ruby was another white person. Tribal allegiances, Ruby reflected, were a weird thing.

Ruby walked, dizzy from the loud traffic, looking forward to the solace of The Hole, where all the city's noise came to die.

Coleman was standing in front of the barn with his bay gelding Captain, surrounded by half a dozen kids. Ruby had completely forgotten it was a kid day. The men and women who kept horses at The Hole volunteered teaching horseman-ship to neighborhood kids. Lately, Coleman had started ask-ing Ruby to help him out, and the whole thing made her nervous. Unlike some of her girlfriends, Ruby didn't have any pressing need to have kids. She figured one day a stray kid would find his or her way into her life and that would be fine. But she wasn't the type who went out of her way to spend time with kids. These kids were all right though. Degenerate little savages whose lives had already been filled with so much hell that nothing scared them. They were mischievous, mouthy, and fearless. Ruby liked that.

"Hi," Ruby greeted Coleman.

"Finally," Coleman said. "You were supposed to be here at noon."

"I was?" Ruby squinted.

Coleman squinted back. "What, you forgot? What the hell is wrong with you?"

The kids started giggling. There were six of them. Five boys and one girl. Ruby recognized one of them, Joey, a gangly dark-skinned kid who lived ten blocks away.

"I got a lot on my mind, Coleman," Ruby said.

The cowboy shrugged and handed her Captain's reins.

"Get this girl up on the horse and lead her around some." Coleman indicated a girl of about ten. She had close-set black eyes and cheekbones that could have sliced a salami. She was giving Ruby the evil eye.

"I'm Ruby," Ruby said.

"Alicia," the girl said.

"You been on a horse before?"

"Yeah," Alicia said, sticking her bottom lip out.

"So, you wanna get on or what?" Ruby asked.

"Yeah," Alicia said, jutting her bottom lip out further.

The little girl walked to the left side of the horse then stared up at the stirrup forlornly.

Ruby hoisted her into the saddle. Captain shook his head once, a homage to some distant past when he actually had the energy to make a fuss over a rider getting on his back.

As Ruby led the gelding forward, she could feel Alicia's eyes boring holes in the back of her head. They walked in silence, just the soft sound of Captain's hooves against dirt. Ruby didn't really know what to say to the girl. She hated the way most people talked down to kids, as if they were morons. Alicia had probably seen more inexplicably painful stuff in her ten years than Ruby had in thirty-four.

"You got that big black horse?" the girl suddenly asked Ruby's back.

"What?" Ruby turned to look at Alicia.

"That big black horse in the barn. That's yours?"

"Yup," Ruby said. "That's Jack Valentine."

"How come you got a horse?"

"Someone gave him to me. He used to be a racehorse, but he hurt himself and can't race anymore."

"How come he hurt himself?"

"Running fast," Ruby said.

"Oh. You don't want him to run fast when you ride him?"

"Not that fast," Ruby smiled.

"I wanna ride your horse," Alicia said then. "This one's too slow."

"Captain's just taking care of you. He knows what's what."

"He can go fast?" Alicia was frowning at Ruby.

"Sure can," Ruby said, "but you're not ready for that yet."

"Yes I am!" Alicia protested.

"Oh yeah?

"Yeah."

"Okay," Ruby said.

She led Captain over to the paddock behind Coleman's barn.

Alicia's face clouded. "I can't go fast in here!"

"Trust me," Ruby said. Ruby let go of Captain, and the gelding dutifully walked ahead. Alicia looked happier.

"How do I get him to go?" she asked.

"Sit up straight and just think about trotting," Ruby said.

"Just think about it?"

"Yup."

"I'm thinking about it," the girl said.

"Now very gently squeeze his sides with your legs," Ruby said. "Gently."

The girl's legs didn't even reach halfway down the horse's sides, but Captain knew what Alicia wanted and obliged with a short choppy trot. The girl bounced all over the place and let out a little squeal. Captain took that as his cue to stop trotting.

"That's it?" the girl said.

"He knew you were nervous."

"I'm not nervous."

"Okay, so do it again. Try to relax. Make your body part of his."

This time Captain trotted around the entire periphery of the paddock before pulling himself up and looking at Ruby with that *Can I go home now?* expression.

Ruby patted the old gelding. Captain let out a sigh but Alicia wanted more. Ruby spent another half hour teaching the girl how to ask the horse to stop, start, back up, and walk in figure eights. Captain, gentleman horse that he was, took care of the little girl. Ruby was starting to wonder if Alicia would ever get tired when finally the girl announced she was thirsty.

Ruby walked over, took hold of Captain's bridle, and helped the girl down.

Alicia raced ahead into the barn, and Ruby expected that would be the last she'd see of her. But as she led Captain into the barn, she saw Alicia standing there, clutching a can of Coke and beaming.

"Now what?" the girl asked.

The other kids were all long gone by the time Ruby had shown Alicia how to groom the horse, clean the tack, and pick the droppings out of Captain's straw. Ruby suspected the girl would have stayed there and slept in Captain's stall if they'd let her, but it was close to 6 P.M. and Coleman announced it was time for him to give Alicia a ride home.

"I can come back tomorrow?" Alicia asked, her mouth forming a hopeful *O*.

Ruby realized she'd just helped create another victim of Horse Fever.

———

NIGHT WAS FALLING by the time Ruby finished her chores and went into Jack Valentine's stall to canoodle with her horse for a few minutes. She'd already turned the lights off and could barely see her inky gelding in the shadows. The dim light was soothing. She fed Jack a mint and watched him roll it over his tongue. He even closed his eyes, giving it the ultimate taste test before finally biting down into it.

A slice of yellow moon was rising as Ruby closed up the barn and started walking down the dirt road, heading toward the subway. Triple Harrison was out on his sagging front stoop, smoking a cigarette and staring into space.

"Hey, Triple," Ruby said.

"Where you going?"

"Home."

"Need a ride?"

"Sure, I'd love a ride to the train."

"I'll do one better and give you a ride home. I wouldn't mind some Nathan's fries."

"Really?"

"Really. Let me get my keys."

Triple got up and disappeared inside his house for a few seconds, emerging with a mysteriously overstuffed backpack.

"You gonna camp out at Nathan's?"

"Nah, just needed a few things," he said cryptically.

Ruby didn't press it.

Triple's Chevy Caprice Classic had once been blue but was now dirt-colored. Inside there were empty soda cans, candy wrappers, and, on the floor of the passenger side, a pair of women's panties.

"Triple, you've got panties on your floor."

"She meant nothing to me," he said, smiling. "You're the only one."

"Be that as it may, would you mind putting those somewhere else?" Ruby wrinkled up her nose.

Triple reached down, plucked the panties from the floor, and stuffed them in his front pocket.

"Greta," he said as he turned the key in the ignition.

"Greta?"

"Owner of the panties. Lives in Brighton, hence the backpack. I might stop in and see her. She's an animal psychic." He nosed the car forward, up the little hill and out onto Linden Boulevard.

"Ah," Ruby said.

"Don't be like that."

"Okay," Ruby said.

"Greta told me my mare would like it if I got her a new goat."

Peanuts, the goat that had lived with Triple's mare, had died of old age a few weeks earlier.

"I could have told you that. *You* could have told you that."

"You're such a pessimist," Triple said.

"How does that make me a pessimist?"

"You just don't believe in magic."

"Sure I do. I'm just leery of incompetent animal psychics."

"You're calling my girlfriend incompetent?"

Now Triple looked genuinely pissed off, and Ruby realized she'd gone too far.

"No, Triple, I'm not. It didn't come out right."

"Uh huh," Triple said.

She tried backpedaling. Asked for more details on Greta

the Animal Psychic, but Triple was hurt now and would answer only in grunts.

"I'm sorry. I've had a bad few days, Triple."

"Whatever," Triple said.

Ruby tried to exude niceness for the rest of the ride. She told cute anecdotes about Alicia and Captain, but it didn't help.

Triple looked gloomy as he nudged the Chevy to the curb near Ruby's building.

"Thanks, Triple. I appreciate the ride, and I'm sorry to be such a downer." Ruby scooted closer to him and kissed him on the cheek.

"Please don't hate me," she said.

Triple finally looked at her. "I won't," he said, giving a tiny smile.

7. RATS

Ruby opened the door to her apartment, and Stinky tried to trip her. As she bent down to pet the cat, she smelled something good coming from the kitchen.

"Where were you?" Ed was standing in the kitchen door, holding a giant spoon covered in tomato sauce.

"You're home? And you're cooking?"

"Evidently," Ed said, leaning down to kiss her.

"I was at the barn," she said when the kiss was over.

"Oh. Right," he said, looking down at Ruby's muddy barn boots. "I'm making pasta," he added.

"Nice," Ruby said. She watched Ed stir the pasta sauce. She had told him thousands of times that pasta after 5 P.M. did strange things to her body and made her feel stupid the next day. Ed had either forgotten or didn't believe her since he thrived on late-night pasta in spite of not having any Italian ancestry. Ed was of German and Irish descent. There shouldn't have been any predisposition for nighttime pasta. Unless you factored in the German people's love of Italy. There was a long history of college-age Germans going to Italy to find themselves. Or so Ruby's German ex-boyfriend had once told her.

As Ed tasted the sauce, Ruby tangentially thought about

the German ex-boyfriend, Axel. He had married a Chinese computer programmer moments after he and Ruby had broken up. The Chinese computer programmer had not been fond of Axel's exes, so Ruby hadn't heard from Axel in six years. She missed him slightly, the way she slightly missed most ex-lovers. Attila was the only one she missed violently. The only one who haunted her. Of course, he was the only one who'd been murdered. Ruby had no idea what she'd feel for him if he were still living.

Ruby ate a good portion of pasta and felt it like lead in her belly. She mentally cursed her boyfriend but outwardly smiled. He'd made her dinner.

Ruby did the dishes then went into the living room, where she found Ed on the couch, eyes closed, a *Law & Order* rerun on the TV. As Ruby sat on the edge of the couch, Ed opened his eyes. They were bloodshot with exhaustion.

"Any idea why your shrink's husband is selling that colt?" he asked.

"What?" Ruby feigned complete ignorance.

"I saw Violet earlier. She was acting mopey and didn't want to tell me why. I finally dragged out of her that she'd just finalized a sale on Fearless Jones. I asked her why the hell Jody's husband wanted to sell the horse, but Violet didn't seem to know."

Ruby worked at looking stunned and disappointed. She was all that and more. And on the verge of telling Ed about The Psychiatrist and the leg when Ed reached up, pulled her to him, and kissed her deeply. The Psychiatrist's story could wait.

———

ED WAS LONG GONE when Ruby woke up the next morning. She fed the cats then read a few pages of *Rats* while sipping a cup of very black coffee. Once the caffeine hit, she rolled out her mat and did forty-five minutes of yoga. At the end, she sat in lotus attempting to meditate. But all she could see was Jody's husband's leg floating before her eyes, bloody and ugly. She gave up on clearing her mind, untwisted her limbs, and went into the bathroom to shower. She got dressed for work and pulled her wet hair into a high ponytail in spite of the fact that wearing her hair that way seemed to inspire more catcalling than usual from teenage boys and construction workers, who apparently equated ponytails with slutdom.

Outside, the sky was teal blue and the air smelled salty. Ruby wanted to walk onto the beach and put her feet in the water. She looked at her watch. Seven minutes to eleven. She had time. Sort of.

She crossed Surf and saw Guillotine, the kiddie-park operator, walking his pack of dogs. The Frenchman had three pit bulls, an Australian cattle dog, and a balding Chihuahua.

"Guillotine, hi." Ruby nodded at him.

Guillotine glanced up and grunted. He had grown a beard over the winter. Long gray and ginger hairs curled and swooped all the way to his collarbone. He was thin and unhealthy looking and his blue eyes were small. Still, Ruby was curious about him and sometimes wished he'd talk to her. Not today.

Ruby walked onto the beach. A few old white guys were

wading into the water. A jogger with headphones was running along the shoreline. Some kids were swimming, their mothers sitting on the beach smoking cigarettes. They looked as though they were really enjoying the cigarettes, and it made Ruby want one. She'd been working on a wad of Nicorette gum all morning, aiming at getting through the day without a smoke. But smoking looked so lovely just then. Ruby stared at the pack of Marlboros right there on the beach towel. She hoped one of the women would notice her staring and offer her a smoke. This was a ludicrous fantasy considering the price of a pack of cigarettes.

One of the women felt Ruby's gaze and glanced up. It wasn't a friendly look. Ruby moved on. She walked to the water, took off her red sandals, and waded in. The sea was warm and soft. Ruby saw several Styrofoam peanuts floating nearby and it depressed her. She figured trash was like rats. If you saw a little, it meant there was a lot lurking under the surface. Ruby took her feet out of the water and walked barefoot on the sand for a few paces. After narrowly missing stepping on a shard of glass, she put her sandals back on.

The beach at Coney Island had never been clean, but it seemed to be getting dirtier. Since the zealous Republican mayors of New York City had managed to reduce crime and eradicate the overt sale of drugs in neighborhoods where white people lived, surely they could do something about Styrofoam peanuts in the sea.

Ruby glanced at her watch. She was now ten minutes late for work. She didn't think her boss, Bob, would mind. But she was wrong.

8. WRONG

Ruby climbed the stairs to the museum and found Bob standing in the middle of the darkened front room, frowning. At his feet were dozens of boxes filled with books and Coney Island souvenirs.

"Hi. Sorry I'm a little late."

Bob lifted his frown and aimed it at Ruby.

"Hi," he said without cheer.

"What's wrong?"

"Is there something you're not telling me?" Bob asked. He looked angry. He'd shaved his head recently and his skull was bullet shaped. He usually looked pleasantly deranged, but today he looked frightening.

"Something I'm not telling you about what?"

"You got money problems?"

Ruby squinted. "What? What are you talking about?"

"You know you can be honest with me. I can loan you money if you need it."

"What? Why are you bringing up money?" Ruby glanced down at her clothing, wondering if she suddenly looked impoverished.

"I'm gonna be all right on my own today," Bob said then. He'd stopped looking at Ruby.

"On your own what?" Ruby asked, confused.

"Working. You can go home."

"Go home?" she asked, bewildered. "But we've got that shipment to unpack." Ruby motioned at the boxes.

"It's okay. I'm fine here on my own," Bob stated.

"Why are you asking me about money, Bob? Is there money missing or something?"

He still wouldn't look at her.

"Just go on," he said, waving her toward the door.

Normally, Ruby would have had some fight in her. But not after what had gone on in the last few days. She stared at Bob. He glanced at her then looked away.

"Okay. I'll go." Ruby paused, expecting Bob to recant. He didn't.

"You want me to come in tomorrow?" she asked.

"I'll call you." He turned his back to her.

"Bob." She tried one last time. "What the hell is going on?"

"Just go," he said in a small voice.

"Fine," Ruby said. "If you decide to tell me what's wrong, you know where to find me."

She slowly walked down the stairs, waiting for Bob to call her back. He didn't. She continued down and out to the street. The sky was too blue and the carousel's organ was screaming.

Ruby let herself into her building and climbed the stairs. Ramirez and Elsie's door was open, and she braced herself for interaction. Neither of them was in the kitchen though. Ruby unlocked her door and went inside her apartment. Stinky didn't even come to greet her.

Ruby sank onto the couch and put her head in her hands.

She really needed to talk to Jane. But Jane was presumably sound asleep behind a swath of mosquito netting in her room in Mysore, India. Living without a phone and glad for it.

Ruby toyed with the idea of calling her mother. Her mother didn't believe in psychiatry, analysis, therapy, or even doctors, and though she'd never say it aloud, she'd think it was all Ruby's comeuppance for going to a shrink in the first place. She would listen to Ruby, but she wouldn't know what to say and would be vaguely appalled at the whole thing. And then feel guilty for being appalled. Make a stab at being solicitous. They would both hang up feeling guilty for not better understanding each other.

As soon as Ruby decided not to call anyone, the phone rang.

"Hello," Ruby said, making it sound like *What the hell do you want?*

"Ruby." Jody Ray's voice sounded lifeless.

"Oh. Hello," Ruby said.

"I need help," Jody said.

"You're not the only one."

That shut her up. But she didn't ask Ruby what was wrong.

"This is absurd, Jody. You ask me for help then you kick me out."

"I'm sorry I've been irrational. You'll admit that under the circumstances, it's understandable."

Ruby did have to grant her that much.

"Will you help me look for Tobias?" Jody asked.

A mosquito had gotten in through one of the defective

screen windows and was buzzing near Ruby's head. She started swatting it with last month's *Velo News*. There was almost nothing Ruby hated more than mosquitoes.

"Ruby?"

"There's a mosquito," Ruby said. She knew it sounded crazy. But no one involved in this particular conversation was in a position to judge levels of sanity.

"I'm not sure," Ruby added when The Psychiatrist failed to offer sympathy over the mosquito.

"Not sure about what? About helping me look for Toby?"

"Right," Ruby said. She saw the mosquito land on a *Daily Racing Form* on the end table. She swatted it with *Velo News* but missed.

"All right. I understand," Jody said in a tiny, weak voice.

"What do you want me to do?" Ruby was angry, but she was curious too.

"Help me."

Ruby paused. "Yeah, okay, I'll do it."

"You will?"

"Why not?"

"Well, there are a thousand reasons why not," Jody said.

Ruby interrupted: "It was a rhetorical question."

"Oh. Right."

"What do I do?" Ruby asked.

"You're familiar with the Rockaways?"

"Yeah. Why?"

"I need you to go there."

"You think Tobias is in Rockaway? Where?" Ruby saw the

mosquito again. Back on the bike magazine. She decided to tolerate it and its horrible little disease-carrying body.

"He seems to have bought a house there. I found the deed and some other papers in his safe-deposit box at the bank."

"And why can't you go?"

"I imagine he'll be keeping an eye out for me. Providing this is in fact a self-orchestrated kidnapping. And of course if he has not had himself kidnapped, if this isn't some idiotic scheme, then he won't be in Rockaway at all."

Ruby couldn't think of a single reason not to report her psychiatrist to the relevant governing bodies. Nor could she think of any reason to do what Jody was asking.

The mosquito was still on the magazine.

"Okay. Give me the address," Ruby said.

Lulu, the calico cat, strolled into the living room and flopped down on the floor, exposing the spot of orange fur on her otherwise impeccably white belly.

"Just a moment," The Psychiatrist said.

Ruby heard Jody shuffling papers. Lulu was staring at Ruby, apparently expecting a cuteness award.

Jody recited an address on Beach Seventy-ninth Street. Ruby pictured stubby buildings close to the water. Boats and couches in front yards. The kind of trashy, wild neighborhood that reminded Ruby of what New York City had been like fifteen years earlier, when it was still irreverent and untamable, before Times Square became Disney World, Manhattan a shiny plaything for Young Republicans.

"Are you there?"

"Oh. Yes," Ruby said. Normally, this bitterness over the taming of New York would have been exactly the kind of thing she'd have discussed with her shrink. Not now though.

"You've never been to this Rockaway place?" Ruby asked.

"Been there? I didn't know the bastard owned this dump."

"It's a dump?"

"A hundred and fifty-two thousand does not buy much in the city of New York in this day and age."

Ruby agreed that it did not.

"Why would he buy something out there?" she asked.

"How should I know? He's nuts," Jody said.

"'Nuts' is better than 'mental defective'?"

"Yes," Jody said. "It's a little less jarring."

"Ah," Ruby said.

"Shouldn't you be at work now?"

"I should. But I'm not. It's a long story."

"You didn't do anything rash, I hope."

"No," she said, "I didn't." She saw no point in telling Jody about what had happened with Bob.

Ruby wrote down the address in Rockaway and told Jody she would go over there.

"And you'll have your cell phone?" Jody asked.

"I'll have it. I'll call you when I get there."

"Thank you," Jody said.

"Yeah," Ruby said, "you're welcome."

She hung the phone up. Lulu was still lying there exposing the spot on her belly, but when Ruby tried to rub the belly, Lulu hissed, got up, and ran away to the shoe closet. Lulu had been a stray who'd come in Ruby's window a few years earlier. For months Lulu wouldn't let anyone touch her. She'd eventually gotten more trusting, especially of Ruby, but still wouldn't stand for humans taking liberties like touching her stomach.

Ruby went into the bedroom to put on clothes she could bike in. She loved the ride over to Rockaway, even if, in this instance, it was under peculiar circumstances. Ruby owned full-on bike-geek gear, including bike shorts, space-age stiff-soled biking shoes, a helmet that made her head look like a red acorn, and several brightly colored bike jerseys, but she only wore it when she was going for an all-out training session on her racing bike. For short-distance commutes and pleasure rides, she wore normal human clothing. She put on a pair of cutoffs and some sneakers.

Twenty minutes later, Ruby was about to roll the bike to the door when something made her pause. There was a bad feeling down her spine not unlike the one she'd had moments before finding Tobias's leg in the fish tank.

Ruby went to the living room window and glanced out to the street below. She didn't know what she expected to see, but nothing unusual was going on down there. Some kids were skateboarding across the street. A man and his pit bull walked by.

Ruby took a deep breath, then hoisted the bike onto her shoulder and carried it down the stairs.

It was a lovely blue day for a bike ride, and within a few miles Ruby had almost forgotten this was no ordinary bike ride. She was focusing on keeping a steady cadence while avoiding potholes and rogue pedestrians crossing against the light. The car and noise levels intensified when she reached Emmons Avenue in Sheepshead Bay. She glanced peripherally at fishing boats bobbing on the water, old people walking hand in hand. She pedaled.

Ruby rode along the Belt Parkway bike path for a few miles then turned off to take the bridge leading to the Rockaways. The guardrail separating the bike path from nothingness was only about waist-high and the wind was strong. She pedaled faster, too nervous about getting knocked off the bridge to enjoy the view of the Rockaway peninsula ahead. When she finally reached the other side of the bridge, she had to get off the bike for a few seconds to recover from the minor terror. She gulped in ocean air until she felt better.

Ruby rode down Rockaway Beach Boulevard into the sketchier parts of the peninsula. Along the water, low buildings gave way to ugly high-rises that were either projects or condos—sometimes it was hard to tell. To the left were tightly packed frame houses and tenements. There wasn't much life on the street and the area felt ominous. Ruby reached Beach Seventy-ninth Street, got off her bike, and walked it along the sidewalk, looking at the numbers on the squat, malnourished buildings. Two kids were sitting on a stoop just ahead. They didn't look friendly but Ruby accosted them anyway.

"You guys know where sixteen-seventy is?"

"What?" a little girl snarled at Ruby.

"Sixteen-seventy Beach Seventy-ninth."

"You're *on* Beach Seventy-ninth," a boy said. He was younger than the girl and a little less mean looking. Both the kids were chubby with pale skin and lank brown hair. The stoop they were sitting on was chipped like a prizefighter's teeth.

Ruby walked on. There was a tire shop and a few crumbling houses leading up to where the street dead-ended at the water.

None of the buildings seemed to have numbers, but at the very end of the road was a one-story brown house with a sagging roof. An old wooden rowboat roosted on the patchy grass in front. The only other residential building on the block was completely boarded up. Ruby decided the brown house was the one. She knocked. Nothing. She tried the doorknob. It turned but the door didn't open. There was a lock that didn't look particularly secure. Ruby fished her bank card from her back pocket then paused and looked over her shoulder. There was nothing there but the empty street and, off to the left, the water lapping at the rocky shoreline. Ruby fussed at the lock with the bank card, got it open, and softly pushed the door open.

"Hello?" she called out. The only sound came from some gulls screaming over the nearby water.

Ruby wheeled her bike inside the house and pulled the door shut behind her.

The place was dark and smelled of mold and stale cigarette smoke. A few slivers of daylight fought their way through curtains drawn loosely over two windows at opposite ends of the place. To her right, Ruby could make out the shape of a sagging couch, near it a low table covered in newspapers. She held her breath, listening for tell-tale creaking sounds. The little house was silent. To her left was a tiny dining room, a six-person table taking up most of the space. Ahead was a kitchen. Ruby ran her hand along the wall, found a switch, and flipped it. A bare bulb dangled over a filthy electric stove. Dishes were piled in the sink, and she saw several cockroaches. To the left of a brown fridge was a padlocked door.

Ruby's spine tingled.

She pressed her ear against the padlocked door but heard nothing. There was a key attached to a magnet on the fridge door. She stuck it in the padlock. It worked. She opened the door a few inches then stooped down to feel her way forward. There was nothing but darkness. Then she saw a blur of movement, and there was a whooshing sound as something came toward Ruby. She felt pain over her left eye. She felt herself falling.

9. SAWBONES

Ruby noticed a terrible smell.

"I'm sorry," she heard someone say. She couldn't see and wasn't even sure if her eyes were open. She put one hand on the side of her head. She felt a sticky warmth and knew it was blood.

"I thought you were someone else," the voice said.

Ruby grunted.

"I'd get you some ice for that, but unfortunately I'm having trouble getting around."

As Ruby's eyes focused, she saw a filthy man hunkered on the floor near her. His face was smudged with grease, and he smelled horrible. Ruby never would have recognized him as Tobias if she hadn't expected to find him here.

"You're a patient of Jody's, aren't you?" Tobias asked, as if they were running into each other at a cocktail party. "I met you at Belmont."

"Yes," Ruby said, finding her voice.

"I'm sorry I hit you on the head. I thought you were Miller coming back to hurt me."

"Miller?"

"My kidnapper," Tobias said casually. "What's your name again?"

"Ruby. And why did this Miller kidnap you?"

"I hired him to. Surely Jody figured that out," Tobias said glibly.

"She wasn't quite sure. But suspected."

"Of course he wasn't supposed to cut my leg off."

Serves you right, Ruby thought. Thanks to Tobias's idiotic scam, Violet was being stripped of her best horse and Jody was flipping out. "You must be in pain," she said.

"Terrible, yes. Miller did give me some Percocet. Takes the edge off."

Ruby caught another whiff of Tobias's body odor. It was vile enough to make her eyes cross.

"Are you all right?" Tobias asked.

"My head's spinning."

"You were out cold for a few minutes," Tobias said. "We should get to a hospital."

"Where is this Miller person?"

"That I don't know," Tobias said.

"I'll call your wife, and I'll call us an ambulance."

"No ambulances," Tobias said.

"You're going to get in some legal trouble no matter what. Calling an ambulance won't make any difference."

"I want to go to a Manhattan hospital, and an ambulance will only take us nearby. I just don't trust these outer borough quacks. Miller has already botched me, I'm sure."

"He cut your leg off himself?"

"Oh yes. He's a veterinarian. I suppose he lacks the bedside manner and subtlety of a human sawbones. But he seemed to know what he was doing."

"You watched him cut off your leg?"

"No no." Tobias waved his hand at the absurdity of the notion. "He blindfolded and anesthetized me. But he gave me a very matter-of-fact report on the proceedings as he went along. Ligated the small arteries, sutured the larger ones. He applied something called thromboplastin to the bone cavities to control oozing."

Ruby was revulsed, but Tobias seemed to relish the telling.

"He was very thorough," Tobias said cheerfully, "and he left me that book so I could acquaint myself with postoperative stump management." Tobias was motioning toward a book on the floor.

Ruby glanced over. *Emergency War Surgery.* A lugubrious-looking burgundy book with gold embossing.

"I haven't been able to focus my eyes to read it though," Tobias added.

Ruby was aghast. "Why exactly did he cut your leg off?"

"I was concerned that Jody wouldn't take the whole thing seriously and wouldn't pay up. Miller thought that leaving her a piece of my body would be a good convincer. I was unsuccessful in talking him out of that particular course of action."

Ruby gulped and stole a glance toward Tobias's leg. Just under the knee, where the leg now ended, Miller had attached some sort of metal device that was pulling the skin over the stump like a sausage casing.

"Now, could we get a car service and go to a hospital, please?" Tobias asked.

"My doctor works out of New York Hospital. Will that do?" Ruby asked.

"That's fine."

Ruby felt for her phone in her pocket then realized she'd put it in the little tool pouch attached to her bike seat.

"Do you have a phone in here?"

"No. Miller took my cell, and there isn't a working phone in the house."

"I'll go get mine," Ruby said.

"Probably won't get a signal. But try it."

Ruby slowly got to her feet and took a few steps forward. She could feel the blood drying near her left temple. Her vision was slightly blurred, and she had the worst headache of her life. She walked into the living room, where her bike leaned against the wall. She took her cell phone out, flipped it open, and punched in Jody's number. No signal. She moved around the dining room. Nothing. She peered out between the filthy curtains, saw that the street was deserted, and stepped outside. The sleepy sounds of the dead-end street seemed loud, the water lapping violently at the shore, the gulls squawking like chickens. She still couldn't get a signal.

Ruby went back in and turned all the lights on in the kitchen, illuminating the little room where Tobias lay. It was her first good look at him. He was wearing a dirty white button-down shirt and striped boxer shorts. There was a black sock on his lone foot. Ruby wondered where the second sock had gone. It hadn't been on the foot in Jody's fish tank.

Tobias was looking at Ruby apologetically, trying to pull his shirttail down over his boxers.

"Don't worry about it," Ruby murmured. She couldn't help but stare at the horrid stump of a leg. For a second, Ruby thought of her friend Cathy, who had dated a long line of men with missing parts. There was a one-armed guy, a guy with one testicle, and an elderly gentleman with only one kidney. Last Ruby had heard, Cathy had settled with a one-eyed man.

"Ugly, huh?"

"That doesn't look good," Ruby conceded. "I can't get a phone signal. Any suggestions?"

"There's a car service not too far away. You could walk over and ask them to come."

"Where?"

Tobias told her. His speech was strained, and as he spoke, he fumbled for something at his side, eventually producing a container of pills.

"Hurts." He put a tablet in his mouth.

"You want some water for that?"

"No," he said. "Don't leave me here too long," he added, seeming weak and needy for the first time.

"I won't," Ruby said. "I'm going to clean up a little," she motioned to her forehead.

"Bathroom's just off the living room."

As Ruby ran water in the sink, she looked at herself in the mirror. There was blood drying around a gash on her forehead, her hair was matted, and the skin around her left eye was beginning to swell and turn blue. She dabbed water onto the wound and saw that it wasn't particularly deep, just tender. She opened the medicine cabinet. Nothing there but a dead roach and a nasty old toothbrush. Ruby wet her fingers and ran them through her hair. She looked like an extra from the zombie movie *28 Days Later.* She flicked off the bathroom light, went to the door, and walked outside.

An old Puerto Rican man was standing in front of the tire shop a few doors down. He stared at Ruby, and she realized she still looked like she'd had an argument with a hammer. She smiled at the man. He didn't smile back.

As she walked, Ruby passed by the pair of kids she'd seen on the way to Tobias's shack. They were still sitting on the stoop, their moon faces blank.

The car service was in a tiny hole-in-the-wall on a deserted side street. The front office was barely bigger than a phone booth. An old man sat hunched behind a bulletproof partition reading a magazine. His head was tilted down, showing a luminous bald spot with a network of tiny blue veins.

"Hi," Ruby said.

The man didn't look up. A phone started ringing. Ruby wondered if the man was even alive.

On the eighth ring, the man reached for the phone, answered, and scribbled something down. He finally glanced up at Ruby and immediately focused on her forehead.

"I need to get a car. Quickly," Ruby said, sticking her chin in the air, trying to act as if a gashed forehead was the most normal thing in the world.

"Where to?" he said after a long pause.

Ruby told him she was going to New York Hospital, in Manhattan.

"Gotta make a stop first on Beach Seventy-ninth and pick up my friend," she said.

The man didn't seem happy about any of it, but he eventually conceded that if she'd wait outside, a car would be ready in five minutes.

Ruby went to stand outside. She pulled her phone out and finally got a signal. She dialed Jody's number. It rang then went to voice mail.

"This is Ruby. I've found Tobias. At the house in Rockaway. He's not in very good shape, and neither am I. We're going to the hospital now. Could you please call me back immediately?" Ruby flipped the phone shut.

A white Lincoln Town Car pulled up to the curb. The driver was a young woman with curly red hair.

"What happened to you?" she asked as Ruby settled into the backseat.

"Fell," Ruby said.

"That ain't from no fall. Someone beat you up?"

"Sort of. Thought I was someone else," Ruby said.

The woman grunted. They drove the few blocks to Tobias's house in silence.

"I have to go in and help my friend walk out. He's sick," Ruby said as the car pulled over. She enjoyed the vast understatement.

The driver grunted again.

Ruby went inside the moldy little house, calling out to Tobias as she opened the door.

There was no answer.

"Hey, Tobias?" Ruby walked back through the kitchen and into the little room where she'd first found him. The room still smelled like him, but he wasn't there.

"Hello?" Ruby called out.

Nothing.

"Shit," Ruby said aloud. She went back into the living room and sat on the couch. She put her head in her hands.

Ruby wasn't sure how many minutes passed, but eventually the driver came in looking for her.

"What's going on here, lady?"

"Sorry," Ruby said, "my friend seems to have disappeared."

"You gonna pay me or what?" the driver asked, folding her arms over her chest.

She was very short, which Ruby hadn't noticed before.

"I guess I still need to go to the hospital," Ruby said.

"You guess? Woman, you definitely need a hospital," the driver said. "What's the problem? You got no money?"

"No," Ruby protested, "I have money."

"I can give you a ride for free." The driver didn't seem to believe Ruby.

Ruby was touched by the gesture but also a little concerned. Apparently, she looked a lot worse than she realized.

"I appreciate that," Ruby said softly. "I can pay you though. I'd like to go to New York Hospital. In the city."

The driver whistled through her teeth.

"You know you're talking forty bucks there, missy."

"That's fine," Ruby said.

"All right," the driver shrugged, "it's your nickel."

Ruby tried to gather the strength to stand up.

"What's the matter?" the driver asked.

"Nothing," Ruby lied. She forced herself to stand. She wobbled a little.

"Whoa, Nellie!" The driver came to Ruby's side and steadied her.

"I need to get my bike in the car." Ruby pointed at the brown bike.

The driver shook her head. "No, no bikes."

Ruby felt her bile rising. It was amazing how much anti-bike sentiment existed in the world, and while Ruby wasn't a total maniac about trying to enlighten others about the wonders of the modern velocipede, neither did she appreciate stupid rules about where bikes could and could not go.

"I'll take the wheels off," Ruby said.

"I don't care if you take the whole thing apart. It ain't coming in my car."

Ruby was too woozy to go in for a big bout of bicycle advocacy. She needed a doctor, not a fight. She pulled the door to Tobias's house closed behind her, followed the driver over to the Lincoln, and got into the backseat. As they drove over the Marine Parkway Bridge, Ruby called Information, got her doctor's number, called his office, and got through to his secretary, Joanne.

"Just have the triage nurse call up to us when you get to the emergency room," Joanne said, unfazed.

Between getting stepped on or bitten by horses and occasionally crashing her bike, Ruby was in to see Dr. Parrish at least twice a year with sprains, bites, or minor broken bones. She didn't have insurance, but Dr. Parrish, a long-time Coney Island fanatic, charged Ruby a reduced rate.

Ruby closed her phone and rested the back of her head

against the seat. She closed her eyes and at some point drifted off, coming to when the car stopped. They were outside New York Hospital, and the driver was staring back at her from the front seat.

Ruby produced money from her pocket, tipping the woman extravagantly, as was her custom.

"Sorry I didn't let you bring your bike," the driver said penitently.

"Yeah, me too," Ruby said.

"You gonna be all right walking in there by yourself?"

"I'm fine, thanks," Ruby said.

She wasn't fine. This was clear from the triage nurse's face. Ruby didn't have to wait long before being ushered onto a gurney and whisked back into the entrails of the emergency room.

Dr. Parrish didn't appear until after Ruby had been CAT-scanned and put through a series of monotonous tests involving touching her nose and following a neurologist's finger with her eyes. She'd been wheeled back behind a curtain and was enjoying the slight buzz of the painkillers they'd finally given her when Doctor Parrish materialized.

Doctor Parrish was a middle-aged man of medium build. He had kind eyes and a high, intelligent forehead. Ruby found him beautiful.

"Bad day, huh?" Dr. Parrish said.

"Not the best," Ruby agreed.

She told him what had happened. Sort of. Leaving out a few key details and painting the whole thing as an accident.

"At least I can go home and go to bed now," Ruby said.

"Ruby, we need to admit you for observation," Doctor Parrish said, using the foreboding *we*. Ruby was never sure what the *we* encompassed. *We* was like *they*. Whenever Ruby used *they*, Ed invariably asked, "Who's *they*? The Van Patten Family?"

"I can't afford a night in the hospital. You know that," she told the doctor.

"I'm sorry, Ruby. It's just a precautionary measure."

Ruby knew that he couldn't advise her to leave.

"I'll check on you in the morning," he said, even though Ruby knew that *he* knew she wouldn't be there in the morning. "Try to stay out of trouble, will you?"

Ruby smiled weakly as Doctor Parrish vanished beyond the curtain.

The hospital smelled of sickness and cheap sheets, and the glare of overhead fluorescents seemed designed to provoke migraines. All the same, Ruby didn't hate hospitals the way most people did. They were places where fascinating and brutal things happened in high concentrations. But she couldn't afford to spend a night there as a sociological experiment. She sat up and put her feet on the floor. After a few minutes, she stood. She noticed she was wearing a hospital gown and, with effort, bent down to look under the stretcher, where she found a bag containing her clothes. She pulled it out and stood back up, getting a head rush in the process. As she dumped the clothes onto the bed, she realized that strangers had stripped her and she didn't remember it happening. She got dressed then pulled the curtain back. Nurses and orderlies were bustling down a hall lined with stretchers and IV poles. Ruby spotted a bathroom across the hall and went in to fix herself up.

Her left eye was swollen and bruised, and a big gauze bandage was covering most of her forehead. Someone had pulled her hair back into a ponytail, but there was still blood matted near the hairline. Her lips were dry and chapped, and on her cheek there was a little cut that she didn't remember seeing before. Ruby washed her hands and patted her face with cold water. She emerged from the bathroom, looked up and down the hall, and then started walking. At the end of the hall, she found a door leading to the stairs. She went down slowly, holding on to the railing. Her head felt heavy on her neck, and she had to concentrate on where she put her feet.

Ruby reached the lobby and walked to the revolving doors that spat her onto the street.

The day's brightness was fading, casting bawdy pink light over the traffic snaking its way down York Avenue. Ruby stood at the curb, waiting for the light to change. Her vision was blurry and she was weak. She leaned against a signpost as she dug her phone out and dialed Ed's number at the barn. He picked up on the fifth ring.

"Yes," he said, sounding cold and businesslike even though he must have known it was Ruby calling.

"Hey, it's me."

"What," he said.

"What's wrong?"

"Nothing. I'm busy."

"Oh." She waited for Ed to say something more.

"Where've you been all day?"

"You'll never believe what happened to me."

"Why not?" His voice was ice.

"What's wrong, Ed?"

"I'm not gonna make it home tonight."

"What? Why? Is Juan okay?"

"Juan's okay. I just won't be coming home."

To Ruby's horror, Ed hung up on her.

She stared at the phone.

Horns honked, pedestrians cursed, and the sky darkened. Ruby dialed Ed's number again. It rang eight times then went to voice mail. She clicked her phone shut and sat down, right on the curb of the busy avenue. She fumbled for the cigarette pack in her back pocket and lit up.

"Are you all right?"

Ruby looked up and saw an elderly woman peering at her.

"No," Ruby said frankly.

"I'm sorry. Can I help?"

"Probably not," Ruby told the woman. She smiled but was pretty sure it came out as a hideous grimace.

"Let me get some help," the woman said.

Ruby watched the woman gesticulate at a nearby traffic cop.

"I'm fine, ma'am," Ruby protested. "Really, I'm just having a bad moment but I'm not ill." Ruby stood up. The last thing she wanted was the attention of a cop.

"But, my dear, you look awful. Did they just let you out of the hospital? They shouldn't have."

"They didn't," Ruby confessed. "I couldn't stand to stay in there any longer. I left." Ruby wasn't sure why she was being so frank.

"I understand," the woman nodded, "but you really

shouldn't be sitting on the sidewalk in your condition. Something terrible will happen." There was toughness in the woman's steel-colored eyes.

Ruby slowly stood up.

"Why don't you come with me? I live only a few blocks away." The woman had taken Ruby's elbow.

"Thank you, that's very kind," Ruby said. "But I need to go home."

"Let me help you get a cab then," the woman said. "Do you need cab fare?"

Ruby felt like laughing. Or crying.

"Thank you, I've got money."

Ruby steadied herself against a lamppost as the older woman hailed her a cab.

"You're sure you're all right, dear?" the woman asked as Ruby got in.

"Yes, thank you, you've cheered me up." Ruby offered the woman her brightest smile.

The woman smiled back and gave a little wave as the cab pulled away. It was one of those rare but exquisite New York moments.

The cabbie was a skinny, compulsively well-groomed man in his twenties. He had pictures of Jesus taped along the dashboard. He winced but didn't complain when Ruby told him she was going to Coney Island. She didn't have the energy to apologize for making him drive to Brooklyn. She rested her head against the back of the seat and dozed on and off through the forty-minute drive. She tipped the cabbie over-generously. He thanked her without moving his lips.

Ruby let herself into the apartment. Ed wasn't there, and the cats didn't even deign to emerge from their sleeping places to greet her. She went into the bathroom to wash up and stared at herself in the bathroom mirror. She looked like total shit. Felt like it too. She was, she reflected, *morbidly alone.*

Ruby came out of the bathroom and went to look at the answering machine. No one had called. I am *morbidly alone,* Ruby thought again. She figured if she kept thinking this ridiculous phrase over and over, it would become so funny she wouldn't feel alone anymore. She tangentially thought of an article she'd read years earlier about the singer Carnie Wilson, who had been *morbidly obese* and had radical surgery to shrink her stomach. "I am so fat I could die," the singer had said before having her stomach surgically reduced to the size of a peanut.

Ruby picked up the phone and dialed Ed, but both his cell and office phones went to voice mail. She tried Jody with the same result. She then plodded into the kitchen and mechanically prepared the cats' dinner. The furry sociopaths emerged from their hiding places. As they ate, Ruby sat at the kitchen table and stared at them.

It wasn't that late, but Ruby was that tired. She went into the bedroom and crawled into bed fully clothed. She pulled the sheet up over her head.

10. MACHINERY

When Ruby woke, it was still dark but everything seemed bright. She got out of bed slowly, wobbling as she took her first steps. She put a hand to her head and touched the bandage. It felt crusty. She hobbled into the bathroom and saw that her eye was swollen and blue. What's more, she was still morbidly alone. She considered jumping out the window. It was only two flights down though. She'd damage herself only enough to make life rotten and difficult.

Ruby went into the kitchen and avoided thinking as she brewed coffee, fed the cats, and downed eight ibuprofen tablets. She pictured the pills eating through the lining of her empty stomach.

As she sipped her coffee, Ruby gazed out at the subway platform. Its metal lines glowed against the still dark sky. As a kid she'd imagined the subway was limitless, that she could get on and stay on, traveling through various states and countries to the very end of the world, where she would get out and sit with her legs dangling over the edge.

Ruby poured a second cup of coffee then went to sit at the computer. She was hoping for e-mail from Jane. Or any piece of good news. There was one note from her friend Elizabeth, asking if Ruby wanted to have dinner sometime. There were half a dozen offers for painkillers and Asian escort services, but that was it. No Jane. Ruby trolled around online, read a little bit of that day's *New York Times,* then went to craigslist and looked at bikes for sale. The last thing she needed was another bike, but she couldn't help looking. Thankfully, there was nothing tempting. Ruby was about to quit her browser when she started feeling extremely sick to her stomach. She got up and went into the bathroom. She vomited bile into the toilet. There was a reddish hue to the vomit, but it was probably just dye from the ibuprofen. She hoped.

Ruby didn't feel much better after the sun came up. Her stomach had settled and she'd eaten some Cheerios, but she felt paralyzed. She wanted to call Ed but couldn't bring herself to do it. She'd started speculating about where he'd spent the night. She pictured him on the narrow cot in the tack room then pictured him in a big fluffy bed with some random buxom vixen. This thought made her nauseous all over again, and she was trying to make herself think something less harrowing when the phone rang. She picked it up, hoping it was Ed or at least her boss Bob, explaining himself.

"Yes?"

"Ruby?"

"Yeah?" It wasn't Ed. Or Bob.

"This is Tobias."

"Where the hell are you?"

"Sorry, I had to go."

"Go?"

"I'll explain eventually."

"What do you want?"

"Just wanted to let you know I'm all right."

"Yeah, I was losing sleep over it."

"Well you don't have to be snotty."

"Yes, I do. I have to go now," Ruby said. She hung up.

She was angry from head to toe. She picked the phone back up and dialed her boss's number.

It rang twice before Bob picked up, sounding irritated.

"Yeah?"

"Bob, it's Ruby."

"Yes," Bob said in a dead voice.

"Should I come into work?"

"No, Ruby, you shouldn't. You're fired," he said before hanging up in her ear.

"That went well," Ruby said aloud, for the benefit of the cats and the dead people. She always figured her dead friends and family were watching on some level, though if she really thought about it, dead people probably had better things to do than tune into her frequency on a regular basis.

When things got particularly shitty on the inside, Ruby forced herself to look good on the outside. She opened the closet and started pulling things off hangers. A crazy flouncy red and white polka dot dress that made her look like a child hooker, a cotton pin-striped Agnes B. suit that made her look like William Burroughs. She selected a vaguely hippie-ish mauve button-down shirt and a pair of lightweight black cotton pants. She put these on but didn't feel even remotely better, and now Cat and Aloisius, Ed's cats, had decided to take up a vigil on the bed. Both were staring at her. Glaring at her. Accusatorily, she was sure.

Ruby felt insane.

She put keys, wallet, and Fireballs into her canvas messenger bag and left the apartment. Ramirez's door was open, but neither he nor Elsie was in the kitchen. Which was just as well.

Ruby walked the three blocks to the lot where her robin's egg blue Mustang lived. It usually took her a few days to build up the courage to drive, but she had to get her bike out of Tobias's house, and she felt compelled to do it now. She didn't want anything of herself left behind there, wanted to be free and clear of Tobias, Jody, all of it.

Emilio was on a chaise longue on the sidewalk in front of the parking lot. He was wearing sunglasses and on his chest was a sign reading PARK HERE. The sign wasn't visible until you stood right near him, so it probably wasn't doing much to drum up business.

"Emilio," Ruby said, looking down at him.

Emilio was apparently sound asleep. Ruby's voice startled him, and he nearly fell off his chair.

"Huh?" He looked at Ruby. His short black hair was sticking up, and his light brown skin had a red, sunburned hue.

"I'm the girl with the 1974 Mustang," Ruby said. Emilio looked as if he had no idea what she was talking about.

"Ruby? Blue Mustang?" She scanned the lot and saw her car parked in a far corner, wedged behind some nondescript vehicles. "There," Ruby said, pointing to her car.

"Oh!" Emilio got to his feet. "Sorry, lady, I was sleeping. What happened to your head?" He motioned at Ruby's bandage.

"Fell off my bike," Ruby said. "That's why I'm driving today."

Emilio shook his head as though bike riding was some thoroughly insane pursuit. When he suddenly realized how much work it would take to get the Mustang out, he lectured Ruby about giving him a few hours' notice before coming to get her car.

Ruby tried to look apologetic.

She nosed the Mustang out of the lot and saw that Emilio was back on his chaise longue, eyes closed.

She got onto the Belt Parkway and considered praying even though her only sense of religion was a vague paganism investing all things with small gods. By the time she reached Tobias's dead-end street, Ruby was almost calm from focusing so hard on the road. She pulled the Mustang up onto the patch of dirt in front of Tobias's house.

The sky was slate gray, and half a dozen gulls circled overhead. Ruby got out and knocked on Tobias's door. She wouldn't have been shocked if Tobias had suddenly rematerialized there in his house. There was no answer though. She tried the door, and it opened, unlocked as she'd left it.

"Hello?" Ruby called out, not expecting an answer.

"Who the hell are you?" a voice asked.

Ruby jumped halfway out of her skin then flipped around and saw a man sitting on a chair beside the door. He was holding a gun.

"Who are you?" Ruby asked, heart pumping.

"I asked first," the man said. He grinned a little. His teeth were large and crooked. He had sandy hair, a few days' beard, and dark eyes. He pointed the gun at Ruby.

"I'm Ruby Murphy." Ruby tried to sound calm.

"And what business do you have here?"

"My bike is here." Ruby motioned at her bike leaning against the wall near where the guy was sitting.

"Where's Tobias, Ruby Murphy?"

"Last time I saw him he was right there." Ruby motioned toward the kitchen. "I have no idea where he is now. I just came to get my bike."

"And the wife?"

"What wife?"

"Tobias's wife. Where is she?"

"She's missing too," Ruby said.

"You think they reconciled and rode off into the sunset?"

"No idea."

"You're not much help, are you?"

"I'm sorry." Ruby silently vowed that if she lived through this, she would lead a safe and dull life ever after.

"So what the hell are you doing here?" Gun Guy wanted to know. He wouldn't have looked threatening if it weren't for the gun. He was probably in his early forties. A decent-looking guy if you went in for the scruffy, crazy type. "And what happened to your head?" he asked.

"Fell off my bike."

"Oh. That one?" The guy motioned at Ruby's brown bike.

"No. My racing bike." Ruby was starting to almost enjoy her ongoing fib about a bike accident. She was ready to embellish it further. Maybe say she'd actually been racing her bike when she'd crashed.

He wasn't that interested though. "You're friends with Tobias?" he asked.

"More with his wife. Jody. She asked me to stop by and say hello to him."

"I thought you just told me she was missing too."

"She is. But she wasn't yesterday."

"Ah." The guy paused. "Tobias owes me money," he said then, as if Ruby could do anything about it.

"Well I don't know where he is. Please stop pointing the gun at me."

"This bothers you?" He looked down at his gun.

"Yes."

"Okay." He shrugged and tucked the gun into the back of his pants. "Tobias and I had a business arrangement, but it went a little sour," he said conversationally. "I fulfilled my end of the deal, but Tobias didn't uphold his end. And that doesn't make me happy."

Ruby wanted to tell the guy that if he expected to get paid, he shouldn't have cut Tobias's leg off. She wanted to ask him why he'd done it. But she didn't.

"So you're going to find Tobias and shoot him?" Ruby regretted saying it the moment it was out of her mouth. The man had a gun after all.

"Just threaten." The guy smiled, unperturbed, showing off his crooked teeth. "Until he pays me. Providing I ever find the fucker."

"Oh," Ruby said.

"What are you going to do when you leave here, Ruby Murphy?"

His mentioning her leaving here implied he wasn't going to kill her.

"I don't know," Ruby said honestly.

"No use reporting me to the cops," the guy said. "I mean, you can if you want to, but I'd be long gone by the time they got here.

"You're pretty unflappable, huh?" The guy added. He seemed to be admiring Ruby, was looking her up and down as if he'd decided she was a tasty morsel.

"I flap as easy as the next girl," Ruby said. "I'm just containing myself right now."

"Wise girl. Anyway, I wouldn't shoot you."

"Thank you."

"You're welcome. You might as well go. I'm going to get going myself." The guy stood up and pulled his button-down shirt over the back of his pants where he'd tucked his gun.

Ruby hesitated.

"Go ahead. Get your bike and go," the kidnapper said.

She didn't wait to be asked twice. She rolled her bike out to the Mustang, took off the wheels, and stuffed everything into the Mustang's small backseat area. She glanced at the house, saw the kidnapper standing in the doorway. He waved. Ruby smiled weakly, got in her car, and drove.

She found the nearest store, double-parked the car, and ran in to buy a pack of Marlboro Red. She got back in the

Mustang and smoked two cigarettes in a row before she could stop shaking.

Then she headed for Belmont.

———

RUBY PULLED IN the main stable gate and drove over to Ed's shed row. She still felt awful. Belmont wasn't working its magic. Even the sight of the horse laundry drying over the railing in front of Ed's barn didn't make her feel much better. Usually, just having a reason to think the phrase *horse laundry* made her happy. Not today.

Ed was sitting in his office with his back to the door. He was shuffling papers. The army cot in the corner was unmade, and dirty clothes were strewn over it. His hair hadn't been combed in days.

"Ed," Ruby called out softly.

He flipped around as though he'd just heard a ghost. Looked at her the same way.

"What's wrong?" Ruby asked.

He said nothing. She could see him taking in her bandaged forehead. But still, nothing.

"Ed?"

"Why?" he said, "Why'd you do it?" His face was drawn down, sinking toward the earth.

"Do what?"

"You know exactly what."

"You mean Tobias?"

"Tobias? Who's Tobias?"

"Tobias," Ruby protested, "Jody Ray's husband, that Tobias."

"You're fucking him too?"

"What?"

"I'm too upset to talk," Ed said. His green eyes looked colorless.

"Upset? Why? What happened?"

"I can't talk about it yet."

"You have to, or we're headed for a major disaster."

"We're already there." He was looking right through her.

"Tell me what the hell this is about." Ruby's chest was constricting. She'd never seen Ed like this. They'd been through some things before, but he'd never seemed this distant.

"Ruby . . ." He looked down at his feet.

"What?"

"Did you think I wouldn't find out?"

"Find out what?"

"This," Ed said. He reached for a manila envelope and extracted two 8-by-10 photographs. "These were mailed to me here. And they don't make me feel great about our future." He thrust the prints at her.

Ruby glanced at the photographs. There was something familiar in them. Then she realized *she* was in the photographs. With Triple Harrison. Appearing, in fact, to be making out with Triple.

"What the hell is that?" Ruby asked. She felt her mouth fall open. She didn't have the strength to close it.

"Looks like Triple Harrison to me." Ed wouldn't meet her gaze.

"This is some sort of really bad joke." Ruby felt cold all over.

"It's not very funny," Ed said. "Did Triple do this?"

"Of course not," Ruby protested. "Why would he do that?"

"He's always been after you."

"Not seriously. He's just a flirt."

"If it wasn't him, then who? And why?"

"I have no idea," Ruby said. "You don't really think I was making out with Triple, do you?" Ruby was searching his face, looking for the man she trusted and who trusted her.

"I don't know what to think. There was that whole thing last year."

"What whole thing?"

"The jockey."

"Attila?" Ruby was incredulous, "but he's *dead.*"

"That's not what I mean. I mean it happened. You were with him."

"And you, as I recall, were fucking some exercise rider in Florida. We hadn't had the monogamy talk yet. Remember?"

"The exercise rider wasn't serious. She was a distraction while I waited for you to come around."

"Come around? Where did I go? You're the one—you moved to Florida. That put a damper on things, remember?"

"It was my job. I was sent there."

"Fine, but don't blame me for sleeping with the jockey when you were in another part of the country and we hadn't had any kind of talk about what was between us."

"Okay. I guess that wasn't entirely fair," Ed said. He finally looked a little sheepish. "But this has rattled me." He motioned at the pictures.

Ruby was still holding the photos but now dropped them onto Ed's desk as if they were burning her fingers.

"I'd be rattled too. But you believe me, right? I didn't do anything with Triple?"

"No matter what I believe, I need some space," Ed said then.

Ruby was aghast. She couldn't believe anyone still said things like *I need space,* and she really couldn't believe Ed was saying it to her. It was grotesque, clichéd, abominable.

And he hadn't even asked about her head.

"You need what?" Ruby gave him the benefit of the doubt. Maybe she'd misheard.

"Space," Ed said.

"Why?"

"Just do. I'm sorry."

"But aren't you going to help me?"

"Help you what?"

"Find out why someone wants you to think I'm doing something with Triple?"

"I can't."

"It's probably got something to do with what's been going on over the last few days," Ruby said. "Aren't you even going to ask what happened to my forehead? I had to go to the emergency room. I lost consciousness."

Ed narrowed his eyes to slits. "What?"

"I got bashed in the head by Tobias. Jody's husband."

"Why?"

"He thought I was someone else." She launched into the story. Tobias's leg in the fish tank. Jody Ray's selling off Fearless Jones to come up with money for what proved to be a fake ransom. The trip to Rockaway. The kidnapper pointing a gun at her.

"Oh, Ruby." Ed sounded more sad than angry. "Why would you keep that from me?" He actually looked close to tears.

"And I have no job. I got fired," she added, figuring she might as well tell him everything.

"What?"

Ruby told him what had happened with Bob.

"That's bizarre," Ed said.

"I know."

"What have you done, Ruby?" Ed said it softly, standing just a few inches from her.

"Done?"

"It sounds like someone is really pissed off at you."

"I don't know," said Ruby, shaking her head, then stopping since even the slight movement of her head made her dizzy.

"Call me if you're in danger. If anything else happens," Ed said.

Ruby squinted at him. "Call you?"

"I need to take some time away. From you. From us."

Ruby felt her mouth fall open. "Because of those pictures?"

"Those were a catalyst maybe, but no. I need to think through some things, and I can't do that while we're together."

"What the fuck does that mean?"

"Don't get angry."

"Why not?"

"It's a good thing."

"How is your leaving me a good thing? Especially when my whole life has been turned upside down?"

"I'm sorry," Ed said. "I am."

Ruby wanted to kick him. Stab him. Run him over with heavy machinery. But more than anything, Ruby wanted to die. She didn't remember ever actively wanting to die before, but in that moment, she wanted to die. Very much.

Ruby turned and started walking away, expecting Ed to call her back, same way she'd expected Bob to call her back. Bob hadn't. Ed didn't either.

She found herself standing by her car. She hadn't even gotten a chance to tell Ed she'd actually driven. He'd bought her that car. Back when it had seemed that they had a long and lovely future before them.

Ruby got into her car, popped a Fireball, and stared blankly ahead. She thought about selling the car. Taking the money and moving to France. Starting over in some little town the Tour de France passed through. But she didn't speak French.

Her head started hurting. She rolled down the window, spat the Fireball out, then took a bottle of Advil from her backpack, popped two pills dry, then put the car in drive, and headed for The Hole.

11. FALLING

Lorna, a tiny woman who boarded her palomino at the barn next to Coleman's, was trotting her horse in figure eights on the dirt road ahead. Ruby drove slowly so as not to spook horse or rider. She parked in front of Coleman's stable gate and got out, nodding at Lorna. The small woman nodded back. Ruby had never said more than two words to Lorna. Not that she disliked her. There'd never been a reason for conversation. Ruby wondered about that now. About all the missed interactions and conversations in a lifetime. For all she knew, Lorna was the most engaging and brilliant woman on the face of the earth. And Ruby would go through life without finding this out all because she didn't have the energy to talk to the woman.

Ruby unlocked the stable gate and greeted Honey and Pokey, who were camped out there, sunning themselves. Both pits lifted their large heads, stared at Ruby, then put their heads back down. Ruby would hate to be an intruder coming face to face with those two. They were wonderful dogs to the humans they knew but would kill anyone with bad intentions.

Ruby stopped in the tack room to get peppermints from her trunk. Feeding candy to a horse was a cheerful, optimistic thing to do. But Ruby still felt like dying.

Locksley, the barn cat, jumped down from the shelf he'd been sleeping on. He was covered in dust and had cobwebs in his whiskers. He violently bumped his head against Ruby's calves until she got out one of the cans of emergency tuna she kept in her trunk and fed him.

As she walked toward Jack Valentine, the horse shook his head and made faces at Ruby. She gave him his peppermint and watched the effects take hold. His ears were in neutral and his eyes went to half-mast as he rolled the candy over his tongue. He was ecstatic. After he'd crunched the mint and swallowed it all, Ruby buried her face against his neck. The horse stood perfectly still as she relaxed enough to let tears come to her eyes. She'd needed a good cry for months. It wasn't quite the soul-purifying wail she could have used, but it helped. Something shook loose.

Ruby put Jack's halter on and brought him into the aisle. She put him on the cross-ties and contemplated him for a few moments. He was big. And she was going to ride him.

As she started putting tack on him, Jack's ears flicked back and forth, searching out information. By the time Ruby led him out of the barn, he was on his toes, prancing toward a nonexistent starting gate.

Jack shook his head once when Ruby tightened the girth. She lowered the left stirrup and took a deep breath. She had no idea what Jack would do when she got up on his back. Horses were funny that way. You could have an excellent relationship on the ground, but it was a different story once you climbed aboard.

Ruby put her foot in the stirrup and hoisted herself up.

Jack darted to the right a little, but Ruby had expected this. She quickly shortened the reins and took hold of him. She asked him to walk forward. They circled the paddock with Jack looking at everything intently, as though he'd never seen any of it before. Ruby was brittle with tension and it was transmitting to Jack, flowing through him, then coming back at her amplified tenfold. After a few minutes of walking, both horse and rider were stiff with anxiety. Ruby asked him to come to a halt so she could dismount. This was definitely enough for one day.

At this exact moment, one of the neighborhood cats came out of nowhere and darted through the paddock, spooking Jack. Ruby's feet were out of the stirrups, and she was holding the reins loosely. Jack crow-hopped to one side, and Ruby went off the other side. It was a long way down. She landed on her side, coiled in a ball. At least she hadn't landed on her head.

"You okay?"

She sat up and saw Triple Harrison walking toward her.

"I'm fine. Can you get the horse?"

Jack was standing a few feet away, reins dangling, gazing at Ruby with what looked like concern.

Triple took him by the bridle.

"You sure you're okay?" Triple asked as Ruby brushed herself off.

"Yeah," Ruby said. She had never been worse. And her hand hurt. There was blood on her palm where she'd scraped against a small rock.

"Hey, you're bleeding," Triple said.

"It's fine," Ruby said.

She walked over to her horse, lowered the stirrup, and got back on.

Triple went to stand just outside the paddock and wisely kept his mouth shut even though Ruby knew he probably had a whole lot to say.

Ruby and Jack circled the paddock. She was more relaxed now, and the horse responded by lengthening his strides and dropping his head. They went around three times before Ruby dismounted.

"What possessed you to do that?" Triple couldn't contain himself anymore.

"My life is a wreck," Ruby shrugged. She turned her back to Triple and started leading Jack to the barn.

"What's that got to do with anything?" Triple was tagging along at Ruby's side.

"I had to do something drastic. So I rode my horse."

"What happened to your head?" he asked after a few beats.

"Fell off my bike," Ruby said.

"Bike and horse both, huh?"

"Yup."

"Ruby, what's wrong?" Triple asked. They were inside the barn now. Ruby's eyes hadn't adjusted to the dimness yet so she couldn't see Triple very well.

"Wrong?" she asked, as she started untacking the horse.

"You're being distant," Triple said.

"What's with the pictures, Triple?" She didn't really think he'd had anything to do with said pictures, but she was taking a stab in the dark.

"Pictures?" Triple tilted his head. "What pictures?"

"Of you," Ruby said. "And me," she added, dropping her voice.

"You and me?" Triple looked intrigued but baffled.

"Never mind," Ruby said.

"What are you talking about?"

"Nothing. It doesn't matter."

"Oh no you don't. What are you talking about?"

"Incriminating pictures. Of me. With you." Ruby refused to look at Triple. She had gotten her curry comb out and was vigorously working on Jack Valentine.

"But we haven't done anything incriminating," Triple pointed out.

"I realize that. But someone took photos that look in-criminating."

"Why?"

"To piss off my boyfriend, for one."

"They showed them to your boyfriend?"

"Yeah."

"Oh, man." Triple scratched his head. "Why?"

"That's what I don't understand."

"You got enemies?"

"Apparently."

Triple shook his head. "I'm sorry, Ruby. I had absolutely nothing to do with it. I'd never do something like that to you."

"I didn't really think you were behind this."

"You must have. Why ask me?"

"I don't know," Ruby shrugged. "Just checking I guess."

Triple looked offended, and Ruby felt like an idiot. They

fell silent. Triple watched Ruby groom her horse. Then, feeling sorry for Ruby, Triple helped her out with her barn chores. They worked in amiable silence, with the barn radio tuned to some off-the-wall program on WKCR that alternated New Music with obscure, stripped-down hip-hop.

Now and then, Locksley wove between Ruby's legs or meowed at her. In their stalls, the horses munched hay and napped.

It was peaceful, but Ruby didn't feel that way.

When she drove away from the barn two hours later, Ruby knew what she had to do.

12. GAME

"I've watched you guys all my life. I know what to do," Ruby told Glenda, the heavily tattooed, chain-smoking woman who managed the Kentucky Derby horse-racing game at Astroland.

"Honey, watching and doing is two different things," Glenda said.

The ash on Glenda's cigarette was at least an inch long. Ruby stared at it, wondering when Glenda would flick it.

"Anyway," Glenda said, "the only shift I could give you is weekday afternoons. Ain't much action then, and you gotta work your fucking ass off getting people to play."

Ruby insisted this was fine. The fact was, it would be horrible. Ruby wasn't particularly extroverted, and she disliked noise. The idea of spending her afternoons shouting at strangers, trying to get them to play the horse-racing game, wasn't a pleasant one. But Ruby had to work. She'd called Bob again, and in a cold voice he'd confirmed to Ruby that she was fired. Ruby had a small paycheck coming, but that was it. No savings, and the rent was due in two weeks. What's more, Ruby didn't know if Ed was ever coming home or paying his half of the rent.

Glenda's ash finally fell. Slowly, some of it sticking to the front of her pink T-shirt. Ruby watched the woman rub the ash into the fabric of the T-shirt.

"You ain't gonna make shit. You know that, right?" Glenda asked. "Like fifty bucks a day will be a good day."

"I need something to hold me over," Ruby shrugged.

"What happened, anyway?"

Ruby was surprised it had taken Glenda this long to ask. There was a solid divide between people who worked the games and rides and those who worked at the sideshow and museum. The two groups almost never mingled, and it was unprecedented for someone of Ruby's position to come slumming in the proletariat like this. The only reason Glenda was giving Ruby a job was that Ruby had been coming to play her horse-racing game since she was twelve years old.

Ruby tried to make light of Bob's firing her, hinting that it stemmed from a personality clash as opposed to an accusation of thievery.

"So what are you gonna do? Live out your days working at my game?" Glenda asked. She'd lit another cigarette and was squinting at a pack of young girls idling by the balloon game across the way.

"I have no idea," Ruby said honestly. She didn't have the strength to go hunting for a "real" job. She needed money, and she needed it fast. Asking Glenda had seemed her only option.

"Here," Glenda suddenly shoved her microphone into Ruby's hand, "get them girls to come over here and play." Glenda motioned at the pack of girls across the way.

Ruby froze at the idea of shouting into the microphone.

"Come on," Glenda urged.

"Ladies," Ruby said tentatively. None of the girls looked her way. "Horse-racing game, ladies, two dollars to play." Ruby got louder: "Every game a winner, two dollars any prize on the table." Ruby picked up one of the immense teddy bears and brandished it above her head the way she'd watched Glenda and others do for so many years.

"You out of your mind?" Glenda hissed at Ruby. "You can't give out no jumbo prize unless you got at least ten players."

"I can win that bear?" One of the girls had sauntered over.

"Yes, you can," Ruby said. "I'll take it out of my own pocket," she whispered to Glenda.

Glenda shrugged and started collecting money from the girl and her three friends. Glenda flicked the switches, activating each of the berths, as Ruby showed the girls how to practice rolling the small plastic balls forward and into slots.

"Get your ball in the red slot, moves your horse three jumps, blue is two, and green is one. Remember, one ball at a time or you're gonna get 'em jammed," Ruby said, getting into the flow. She'd heard Glenda and others do this speech so many dozens of times, but she never realized she'd memorized the damn thing.

"Hold on to the balls, ladies." Glenda's double entendre was lost on the girls. "At the sound of the bell, start rolling. Sound of the bell," Glenda said, then depressed the bell and the game started. One of the girls, a tiny, dark-skinned girl in a bright green outfit, was hurling the balls so violently they were popping out of her berth, and Glenda went over to scold her. Meanwhile, the apparent leader of the pack, a big girl with bleached-blond cornrows, was hitting one after another red slot, making her mechanical horse valiantly lurch forward. She won by many lengths, and before Ruby could hand her the bear, the girl was tearing it from Ruby's arms.

"What do I owe you?" Ruby asked Glenda, digging into her pocket to find the small wad of cash she had there.

"Ah, it's all right, Ruby. Just don't do it again. Minimum ten players before you give out the jumbo."

Ruby nodded then bummed a cigarette from Glenda. The two smoked in silence until another pack of kids walked by. Ruby watched Glenda entice them with promises of prizes and fun. They were teenagers with hard eyes that softened fractionally as they rolled the little balls into the slots.

Ruby hung around for more than an hour, learning the ropes.

"I know you ain't gonna be doing this long. Just don't leave me hanging when you decide to quit, y'hear?" Glenda said before Ruby left.

Ruby vowed to give notice when the time came. Glenda patted Ruby on the back and sent her on her way. She slowly walked toward home. It was almost unbearably humid, and people were streaming toward the boardwalk carrying coolers, towels, and boom boxes. An attractive Puerto Rican couple walked by, the man adoringly stroking the woman's head as they walked. Ruby felt her chest constrict.

As she passed the sideshow, Ruby looked over to see if Bob was hanging around the way he sometimes did before the sideshow opened for business in the evening. He wasn't. But

FLAMETHROWER

Lucio, the fire-eater, was lying on top of the little platform out front, apparently napping.

"Can't say hello?" he called out as Ruby walked by.

"Hey, Lucio, thought you were sleeping," Ruby said.

Lucio sat up and smiled his slow, enticing smile. He had medium brown skin, green eyes, and reddish hair that he kept cropped very short, presumably so he wouldn't burn it off. Ruby liked watching him in the sideshow and had particularly relished the times when he'd filled in for the escape artist. She'd savored the sight of Lucio dangling by his ankles from the ceiling, working his way out of a straitjacket.

"What's up?" Lucio asked. He had inched to the edge of the wooden platform so he was very close to where Ruby was standing. She saw his eyes going to her forehead, but he didn't ask about it.

"Nothing," Ruby shrugged. She wondered if Lucio knew about her being fired and accused of theft.

"What are you doing now?" Lucio was looking at her like she was a Christmas ham.

"Going home." Ruby motioned toward Stillwell Avenue.

"Want to have dinner?"

Ruby admired the way he'd just come out with it.

"I can't," Ruby said. She wasn't sure why she couldn't. It was an automatic response.

"You married to that tall guy I seen you with?"

"He's my boyfriend," Ruby said.

"Lucky guy."

Ruby was at a complete loss over what to say or do next.

She smiled weakly. "See you around," she said as she walked away.

"I hope so."

Ruby could feel his eyes boring into her back.

As Ruby came within a few steps of her building, she felt eyes in her back again. She turned around suddenly and saw a man in a baseball cap a hundred yards behind her. For a moment they locked eyes; then the man turned and walked the other way. There was something horribly familiar about him, yet Ruby couldn't place him. A chill passed through her even though it was 90 degrees outside.

Ruby let herself into the building, looked back once more to make sure the man was gone, and walked upstairs. She'd never been so glad to see Ramirez's door open. Even better, Ramirez himself was nowhere in sight, but Elsie was sitting at the kitchen table, sipping tea.

"Oh my god, what happened to your head?" Elsie rose to her feet and waddled toward Ruby.

"Hey," Ruby said, gladly accepting Elsie's hug. "Accident."

"What kind of accident?"

"If you make me some tea, I'll tell you," Ruby said. Elsie was always trying to get Ruby to drink tea but rarely succeeded.

"That bad?" She knew it had to be if Ruby was accepting the tea offer.

"Yeah, I guess it is that bad." Ruby sank down into one of the kitchen chairs.

"Tell me." Elsie put the kettle on and sat down across from Ruby, who started reciting the events of the last week.

Elsie would now and then interject "Get out of here" or

"No way." When the kettle started whistling, Elsie got up. She motioned for Ruby to keep talking as she poured hot water into an old-fashioned teapot. Ruby brought Elsie up to the present and her new position as a worker at the horse-racing game. This seemed to upset Elsie more than anything else.

"I don't know why you don't just ask Pietro for a job."

"We're neighbors. No good. If he got mad at me, it would be awful. I'd feel hostility radiating through the walls."

"How's he gonna get mad at you working in a fun-house, girl?"

It had crossed Ruby's mind to ask Ramirez for a job working at the Hell Hole, the spook house he'd owned and operated for the last five years. But Ramirez was a little volatile, prone to getting furious with his employees. The last thing Ruby wanted was animosity from her neighbor.

"I'm fine working for Glenda."

Elsie made a face. Glenda wasn't known for her sparkling personality.

"And I'm gonna kill that fucking boyfriend of yours," Elsie added.

Normally, Ruby would have defended Ed's honor, but this wasn't normal. She said nothing. She finished her tea, refraining from commenting on exactly how bizarre it tasted.

"I should go." Ruby rose from her chair. "Gotta feed the cats. Thanks for listening."

Elsie looked at her with pity. "Oh, baby," she said in that warm way that only nonwhite women seemed able to pull off. Had Jane or Ruby's friend Elizabeth said "Oh, baby," it would have just been weird.

"I'll be all right, Elsie," Ruby said, taking a few paces toward the door. "Thank you." She smiled at her friend.

The apartment had never seemed so depressing. Maybe because it never had been. When Ruby had moved in four years earlier, she'd been starting fresh after nearly drinking herself to death. A stint in a Texas rehab had detoxed her enough to make her realize she wasn't happy in Texas. She'd moved back to her native Brooklyn. She hadn't had much in the way of needs and was just damned glad to be alive. That she'd ended up getting the museum job and liking both her job and her boss had been almost shocking after a long series of menial, meaningless, and thoroughly unpleasant jobs. As months passed, Ruby got used to living comfortably. She lived a simple, almost childlike existence and had no interest in acquiring the big problems and stresses that came with big careers and big lives. When Ed had come along, he'd seemed like crowning glory in an already good life. But now that he was in the wind, that life didn't seem so rich anymore, and the simple things that had once made Ruby happy seemed useless and slightly pathetic.

She went over to the stereo, put a Joy Division CD on at full volume, and lay down on the floor.

After four songs, Ruby got up, swapped Joy Division for Bach's *Well-Tempered Clavier,* then went into the kitchen to feed the cats. All four were at her feet, staring and meowing, and as she fed them, Ruby started fuming. Ed apparently assumed she'd take care of his two cats. Ruby stormed back into the living room, picked up the phone, and called Ed. Of course he didn't answer. She gave his voice mail a piece of her mind about abandoning cats, even though it had been only forty-eight hours and this probably didn't technically constitute abandonment.

"I hate that you've assumed I'd take care of your cats. I hate assumptions. And I hate whatever it is you're doing."

Ruby hung up but felt not one iota better. She turned the music off and went to her piano, where she banged around unsuccessfully for twenty minutes. She gave up on that particular path to salvation then decided that if she stood in the house one minute longer she would explode. She put ten bucks and two Fireballs into her pocket and went out. She saw Elsie and Ramirez sitting in their kitchen. She attempted a smile, was pretty sure it came out a grimace, and without waiting to see the grimace's effects went down the stairs two at a time. She jogged down Stillwell, across Surf, and into the Eldorado Arcade, where she got ten dollars' worth of quarters from the change machine and started playing Skee-Ball, compulsively pumping more quarters in the moment she threw the ninth ball of each game.

This didn't help either. Ruby gruffly handed the two dozen prize tickets she'd won to a small chubby child then stalked out of the arcade and headed for the beach.

She felt like she was being crushed.

Weak waves lapped at the shore. The low-hanging yellow moon would have been pretty under most circumstances, but all Ruby could think was that it was yellow from pollution that was all the fault of George Bush, who seemed determined to rape and deplete the earth. Ruby took the opportunity to blame George Bush and his handlers for everything. The Disneyfication of New York City. The dumbing down of suburban America youth, and the ridiculous hypocritical espousal of a religion that forbade stem cell research but was just fine with killing thousands of full-grown humans. It made Ruby's stomach hurt. She was so knotted-up she couldn't bear staring at the dirty water any longer and started slowly walking back toward Astroland.

She hadn't meant to, but Ruby walked by the sideshow, stopping to watch Lucio, who was out front, on the platform, performing a few minutes of his act in order to entice passersby inside to see the full ten-in-one sideshow. His neck was arched back as he swallowed a flame from a wand he held above his head. About a dozen people were standing around him in a semicircle, and nearly all had their mouths hanging open. Eating fire wasn't really that difficult—Ruby had even done it a few times—but Lucio did it so beautifully. And that was difficult.

Ruby didn't want Lucio to see her standing there admiring him. She kept walking.

It was still early, but Ruby put on her red nightgown and got into bed with *Rats* for company. Eventually, sleep came.

13. FIRE

The next few days were a blur, time shifting but barely moving under an orb of swollen sun. In the mornings, Ruby went to The Hole, spent time with her horse, and did her chores. Afternoons, she went to bark at strangers at the horse-racing game. Some days she worked with Glenda, others with Glenda's son, Rafael, a lecherous muscle head who was always trying to look down Ruby's shirt even though Ruby wore sports bras.

Ruby didn't exactly get a lot of joy out of her work at the game. It vaguely fulfilled the fantasy Ruby had shared with many kids about running away and joining the circus. Mostly though, it was tedious and loud, and Ruby would go home with her bones hurting.

Five days into her stint as a game worker, Ruby got a letter from Ed: "Sorry about the silence, and thank you for taking care of the cats. Here's some money for their upkeep. I'll be in touch soon."

She punched the wall so hard she broke the skin on her knuckles and scared the cats. Her hand hurt afterward, and both piano playing and yoga became painful.

The night after her eighth day working at the horse-racing game, Ruby felt so low she wanted to crawl into a hole and die. She tried to seem normal and friendly to Glenda as the older woman paid her for the day. But even Glenda, who wasn't exactly the intuitive sort, realized something was wrong.

"What's wrong?" she asked as she watched Ruby stuff the cash in her pocket.

"Nothing," Ruby lied.

"Okay," Glenda shrugged, "see you tomorrow."

Ruby stopped in front of the sideshow, glancing up to the second floor where the Coney Island Museum's windows were. She remembered cheerier times when she'd take a chair and park it in front of a window, sit there smoking and staring out at all the bustling of Astroland.

It was close to seven now, and the sideshow was in full swing. Todd, one of the talkers, was outside inciting the masses to come on in and see the show. Ruby went in half hoping that Bob would be there drinking a beer with Eek, the tattooed-head-to-toe performer/ticket taker who was one of the better known denizens of Coney. Bob wasn't there, but, judging by the speculative look Eek gave Ruby, she figured Bob had told everyone that he'd fired her from the museum. Thankfully she was long past caring.

"Gonna watch the show," she told Eek as she walked by the desk where he sat selling tickets. She was mentally daring him to charge her admission. Eek wisely didn't take her up on it.

Ruby found a seat in the bleachers. Doriana, the snake charmer, was onstage, a pair of albino pythons writhing over her light brown body as the audience sat rapt and very possibly horny. Doriana was followed by Bubbles, a thin, fortyish white man who drove nails up his nose and swallowed a sword, causing kids in the audience to erupt in grossed-out choking sounds. Finally, Lucio appeared. This is what Ruby had come for: eye candy. He was dressed in loose black pants and a tight black T-shirt. He grinned at the audience, then lit his torches and began arching his neck back, swallowing the flames. He had a beautiful neck. Objectifying the fire-eater made Ruby feel better than she'd felt all week. When Lucio finished, she got up and climbed out of the bleachers, heading for the exit. She was about to leave when the fire-eater materialized at her side.

"Thanks for coming to watch me," he said.

"A pleasure." Ruby pictured herself taking his clothes off. He was lean. He had long lovely muscles. Young skin.

"Come on." Lucio motioned for Ruby to follow him. Since she could think of no reason not to, she did.

They walked in silence toward the beach. Night was coming on, dark overhead, pink at the edges. There were few people on the beach. A helicopter was passing, shining a searchlight at the sea, and Ruby idly wondered if someone had drowned of if contraband had floated to the surface.

Lucio took off his T-shirt, put it on the sand, and motioned for Ruby to sit. She glanced at his hairless chest.

"What's going on with you?" He asked it the way an old friend would. Matter-of-fact, implying it was natural for him to notice she wasn't quite right. He touched her face. "Come on, tell me."

"Too much to explain."

He nodded and looked away. A couple walked by hand in hand. Lucio started fumbling through his pockets. Ruby suddenly wondered if he was looking for a condom. Then decided this was an insane thing to wonder. She wished it weren't. She wished she could lose herself in this boy. The young skin. He produced a pack of Marlboros and offered her one. She accepted. They smoked.

The sea lapped at the sand.

Ruby found herself resting her head on Lucio's shoulder. She didn't remember articulating the muscles to do this. It was just that her head weighed too much and it found a place on Lucio's shoulder. She closed her eyes and, after a few seconds, felt his fingers on her face, tracing the shape of her jaw. Then his lips were on hers, and she felt herself opening up. She wanted him to fill her up.

She was lying on top of the fire-eater, biting into the beautiful soft skin of his neck. She felt hot and sick and broken. The sea was making its sounds.

Lucio dug his fingers into her forearms, up to her shoulders, under her T-shirt.

"Hey," he said suddenly. He gently pushed Ruby off him and sat up. "Are you gonna use me?" he asked. His mouth was partially open, and she could see the tip of his tongue.

"Use you?" Ruby was incredulous.

"You got a man. I can feel him here between us."

"That man *needed some space,*" Ruby said disdainfully.

"And the way you're mad about it has a hold on you."

Ruby invariably had the misfortune of picking virtuously minded men to try having fix-it flings with. Not that she'd done anything like this in a long time. When things had been going well with Ed, she hadn't had a wandering eye. But things weren't going well with Ed now.

"I like you," said Lucio, "but I don't want you when you got your mind on some other man."

"What about sex for the sake of sex?" Ruby asked.

"Aw, come on, girl," he said, touching her lips with his index finger, "you know it's gonna be a mess."

"Define mess."

"Feelings," he said.

She wasn't sure if he meant he'd have feelings, she would, or both, but it was presumptuous of him. And she sort of liked that.

"Why'd you bring me here then?" Ruby asked.

"Seemed like the natural thing to do. Only now that I got my hands on you, I can tell there's something unresolved between you and that tall guy."

Ruby rolled her eyes.

"Don't roll your eyes. You know I'm right."

Ruby shrugged.

"I've got another set soon anyway." Lucio got to his feet then reached down to pull Ruby to hers.

She regretfully watched him pick up his T-shirt, brush it off, and put it back on.

"Cheer up, now we're friends," Lucio said. "And you need a friend right now. I heard Bob fired you."

Ruby let herself smile. "True," she said.

"Hello, friend." Lucio kissed her on the cheek.

"Hello," she said.

"Come on then." Lucio took her elbow and guided her back toward the boardwalk.

Outside the sideshow, Lucio pecked Ruby on the cheek. She watched him walk away. His athletic ass was a thing of beauty.

Ruby was slightly less miserable as she let herself into the building and climbed the stairs. She didn't really care that Ramirez and Elsie's door was closed or that the cats didn't bother to greet her. She put on one of her beloved Einstürzende Neubauten CDs and went into the kitchen. The cats surfaced and she fed them. She stared inside the fridge, willing something palatable to appear. Nothing did. She put a banana, yogurt, and orange juice in the blender and had herself a drinkable dinner. She had just rinsed out her dinner glass when the phone rang.

"Yeah?" Ruby realized she'd taken to answering her phone like an angry person. Probably because, right now, she was an angry person. A depressed loner. A miserable wretch.

"Ruby, it's Tobias."

Ruby felt nauseous.

"You there?" Tobias asked.

"Yes," Ruby said after a long while. "Where are you?"

"Still at large," he said breezily.

"What can I do for you?" Ruby asked, more for something to say than out of any actual will to do anything for the guy.

"Could you help me find Flamethrower?"

"Flamethrower? What?" Ruby thought of the flashy chestnut colt who'd been a very nice racehorse a few years earlier. What the horse had to do with the price of beans, Ruby didn't know.

"My wife," Tobias said. "It's a nickname. Sorry."

"*Flamethrower* is her nickname?"

"Yes. It's a long story."

"Ah," said Ruby. "She still hasn't turned up?" She felt a small ping of curiosity.

"No."

"Does she know where to find you?"

"She has a phone number to reach me, yes."

"You think she's in trouble?"

"Trouble?"

"I mean, is that why you're looking for her?"

There was a long pause. "It's possible, yes," Tobias said. "She had a relapse just two years ago."

"Relapse?"

"You know the cliché about all psychiatrists being nuts?"

"Sure."

"It's a cliché for a reason."

"What are you telling me?"

"Jody has spent time in institutions. Not just as a doctor. She'll be fine for years at a time but then, boom, she relapses."

Ruby was both titillated and appalled. "Why? What's wrong with her?"

"I can't really go into all that right now," Tobias said. "What's more, she has all our money."

"Ah," Ruby said. "Sounds like you're fucked."

"Well put," Tobias said. "But the fact is, I have nothing to live on. I'm hoping to talk sense into my wife's head. If she doesn't want to come back from wherever it is she's gone, then maybe at least she'll give me some money."

"I sincerely doubt that, Tobias," Ruby said coolly.

"Please don't be mean."

"I'm not. Just stating the facts."

"Yes, I suppose," he sounded whimpery.

"How's your leg?" Ruby asked, softening slightly.

"Still gone."

Ruby laughed. "I hope you got medical attention."

"A physician friend is helping me. Stretching the skin of my stump. Thank you for asking."

Ruby was curious about this but didn't pursue it.

"Ruby?"

"Yes?"

"Can you please help me find my wife?"

Ruby took a breath. "Why me? Hire a professional."

"You'll have a better result. Namely that my wife might actually talk to you if you find her. I'll pay you of course."

"With what?"

"I have a little stash."

"Keep your little stash. You're going to need it. Anyway, I'm not qualified to find your missing wife," she added.

"Not what I hear."

"Not what you hear about what?"

"Jody told me you helped nail someone for a horse-killing insurance scam. Genuine private detective work."

"Oh yeah. That was genuine all right. I genuinely almost got killed, and I genuinely have no interest in repeating the experience."

"My wife won't kill you."

"No, she won't. No one will because I'm not doing it."

"Please?" Tobias asked, sounding weak, innocent, and nearly sincere.

Ruby hesitated. She realized she wanted to know where her psychiatrist had gone and why. "Have I piqued your interest?" Tobias asked. "I can wire a thousand dollars into your bank account tomorrow."

"Oh?"

"Yes," Tobias said.

Ruby wasn't in a position to turn down a thousand dollars.

"Okay, I'll do it," she said.

"Really?" He sounded giddy.

"Yes."

"Thank you."

"I don't guarantee any results."

"I understand."

"And you still have to pay me. No matter what."

"Give me your bank's phone number and your account number."

Ruby thought this over for a minute. Wondered if Tobias was trying to steal her identity. Decided there wasn't much to steal.

"Sure," she said. She gave him the information.

"So?" she said after Tobias had written it down.

"So what?"

"Where do I start? Where do you think she is?"

"Oh," Tobias seemed surprised, as if he'd expected to have to beg Ruby to get started. "You should go to our brownstone first. Make sure she's not there."

"How do you want to get keys to me?"

"I don't have them. She's had the locks changed and taken out a restraining order in case I went off the deep end."

"Ah. So. Exactly how am I supposed to get in?"

"I imagine you'll have to call The Crone."

"The who?"

"One of Jody's lovers from years ago. They keep in touch. She's an awful woman. But Jody dotes on her and confides in her. The Crone has keys, I'm sure."

"Ah," Ruby said. Her head was spinning at this information.

"I realize this is more information than you might want about your psychiatrist's past."

"Probably, but I'll live."

Tobias laughed.

"So you want me to call this crone person and ask for keys to the brownstone?"

"Actually, yes, that would be lovely."

Lovely wouldn't have been Ruby's adjective of choice. She wrote down The Crone's phone number and learned that her given name was Millicent.

"I'll have the money in your account by tomorrow morning," Tobias said.

"And how am I supposed to get in touch with you?"

130

"I'll call you," Tobias said. "Thank you," he added before hanging up.

Ruby hung the phone up. Stinky meandered over, opened his mouth, and let out a long, slow meow.

"I know the feeling," Ruby said, running her hand along Stinky's spine. He bumped his head against her legs then wandered off.

Ruby went into the bathroom and threw water on her face. The bruising was nearly gone, but she looked gaunt. She'd probably lost five pounds in the ten days since she'd found Tobias's leg in the fish tank. Normally, she'd be thrilled to dip below her standard 118 pounds. Now, she didn't care. She ran a brush through her hair, trying to talk herself into worrying about her appearance. It didn't work. She walked back out of the bathroom and stared at the phone. She thought about calling The Crone. She pictured a sagging woman with a hook nose. Then revised the image. Surely Ruby's fiery psychiatrist wouldn't have had a sagging, hook-nosed lover. She picked up the phone and punched in the numbers. It rang three times; then a brutish-sounding woman barked "Hello."

"May I speak with Millicent, please?" Ruby used her sweetest voice.

"Who wants her?" the voice asked.

"My name is Ruby Murphy. She doesn't know me, but I'm a friend of Jody Ray's."

"Friend? I've never heard of ya."

"Is this Millicent?"

"Yeah, Millie. That's me."

"I got your number from Tobias," Ruby said.

"What's that fuck doing handing out my number?"

"Jody seems to be missing. Tobias thought you might know where she is."

Millicent grunted. Ruby had to admit, she *did* sound like a crone.

"Tobias seemed to think you might know where she is," Ruby repeated.

"What, and I'm gonna tell him?" Millicent was incredulous.

"We're worried about her," Ruby said innocuously.

"Who's *we*? What are you, his piece on the side?"

"I beg your pardon?"

"Sorry. The guy's a creep. I guess that doesn't mean you are. But who the fuck are you?"

Tobias hadn't mentioned that in addition to being a crone, Millicent was foulmouthed. Of course, Ruby respected a woman who cursed.

"A patient of Jody's," Ruby said in her most reserved voice.

"Oh? And how is it you know the bum?"

"What?"

"Tobias."

"Long story. Listen, could I come see you, talk to you in person? Maybe tomorrow?" Ruby realized she wasn't going to get very far with this woman over the phone.

"I won't keep you long," Ruby added.

"Yeah, all right." The Crone gave Ruby an address up in

Harlem. Ruby wondered what the very white-sounding Crone was doing living in Harlem. Like all of Manhattan, Harlem had gotten gentrified, but it still wasn't where Ruby would have expected her psychiatrist's crone ex-lover to live.

The Crone told Ruby to come at ten. Ruby agreed she'd be there and hung up before Millie had time to change her mind.

Ruby had a hunch the whole Crone thing would take up a lot of time. She called Glenda at home to tell her she couldn't work the next afternoon.

"Glenda, it's Ruby."

"You quitting already?"

She hadn't planned on it, but it suddenly seemed like the best idea in the world. Ruby wasn't even sure she could count on Tobias to come through with that thousand dollars he'd promised, but she decided to risk it.

"Yeah," Ruby said.

"You coming in tomorrow at least?"

"I can't, I'm sorry."

"What happened to that notice you promised you'd give me? Huh?"

"I could try to come in late afternoon," Ruby said, even though she really didn't want to.

"Ah, it's all right. Gonna rain tomorrow anyway. Probably would have sent you home."

"Oh," Ruby said.

"Okay, you're off the hook."

"Thanks, Glenda," Ruby said.

"Don't mention it." Glenda hung up in Ruby's ear.

Ruby went to find Stinky, scooped him into her arms, then deposited him on the bed and crawled under the covers.

———

RUBY GOT UP AT 5 A.M. so she'd have time to do her chores at The Hole before going to see The Crone. She'd had only four hours' sleep and was stiff and tired. She drank two espressos, read a few pages of *Rats,* fed the cats, and left the house. She'd called Emilio the previous night, warning him she'd need her car by five-thirty in the morning. He'd grumbled then said he'd send his nephew, Phil, to get the car for her.

Ruby reached the lot, but it was locked and Phil wasn't there. Ruby foraged through her bag, found her cigarettes, and lit up. Her lungs ached as she inhaled, and the ache felt right somehow. As though doing this to her body would lighten the load on her mind.

To the east, daylight started fringing the sky. Ruby imagined the rides waking up, their long metal wings groaning to life, their elegant skeletons begging for grease before carrying that day's load of fun-starved fiends.

Across the street, the Three Brothers Deli was open, its sickly yellow light the lone beacon on the block. As Ruby smoked, an old man wearing a winter coat and nasty-looking bedroom slippers shuffled inside the deli and started waving his arms around. Ruby couldn't tell what he was shouting, but it must have been threatening. Ruby had just stubbed out her cigarette when a cop car pulled up and two officers, both female, got out. Ruby was considering taking a few steps closer to watch the drama unfold when Phil finally appeared. He was a small guy with jet-black hair and a ridiculously small nose. He was probably young but was one of those people who'd looked old by age twelve.

"Marlon making a stink again?" Phil asked Ruby.

"Huh?"

"Old bum guy in the deli? Wearing a big coat?"

"Oh. Yeah. He's a regular?"

"Oh yeah," Phil said. "I'll get your car," he added, apparently losing interest in the deli drama.

While Ruby waited, she watched the cops escorting Marlon out of the deli. He was still shouting, and one of his slippers was gone.

———

RUBY MADE IT TO The Hole in less than fifteen minutes, and by seven-thirty she'd mucked the stalls, fed Locksley, and groomed her horse. She was putting the wheelbarrow away in the stable yard when Coleman pulled up in his cream-colored Eldorado. The passenger-side door opened, and Honey the pit bull jumped out and trotted toward the barn with remarkable grace considering the fullness of her figure. Pokey, a scary-looking white pit with a head the size of a bowling ball, jumped out after Honey. Both dogs eyed Ruby, decided to remember that Ruby was allowed to be there, then ambled over to the empty stall Coleman had transformed into a deluxe doghouse.

"What are you doing here so early?" Coleman asked.

He was walking slowly, and there was a little hitch in his step.

"I've got a bunch of stuff going on today," Ruby said. "Just wanted to get my chores done in case the day got away from me. You okay?" Ruby motioned toward Coleman's leg.

"My new woman's wearing me down," he said slyly.

"Oh," said Ruby. She briefly envisioned a strapping vixen keeping Coleman prisoner in her bedroom.

"You get on that horse today?" Coleman had actually caught Ruby riding Jack two days earlier. He'd been as pleased as he'd been shocked.

Ruby shook her head. "Not today, no time."

"Why? What you doing now?" Coleman knew a little about what Ruby'd been up to recently, but she didn't feel like explaining that she was on a wild goose chase for her psychiatrist.

"I've got to do a favor for a friend. That's all."

"Uh," Coleman grunted. "Well, I got some horses to ride," he said. He nodded at Ruby and walked into the barn.

———

RUSH HOUR WAS HIDEOUS. Ruby remembered how only weeks earlier she'd vowed never to drive in intense traffic. So much for vowing.

It took close to an hour to get to The Crone's neighborhood, and all Ruby wanted was to get out of the car and stay out. She found a spot on St. Nicholas Avenue. It took her a while to actually park the damned car though. She'd passed the parallel parking portion of her driving exam, but just barely. She was inching the car forward for the fifth time when she noticed a pack of kids on a stoop pointing and laughing at her. When she finally got out of the car, Ruby waved and smiled at them, and they laughed some more.

The Crone's block wasn't one of the more gentrified blocks of Harlem, and it seemed to Ruby that her white face was drawing attention as she walked slowly, looking at the building numbers. It reminded her of the time she and Ed had looked at a crumbling brownstone for sale in the heart of Bedford-Stuyvesant. It was a gorgeous old building with soaring ceilings, ornate moldings, and wide-plank floors. A little bit of hard work would have restored it to its former glory. But as Ruby and Ed walked down the block, everyone stared at their white faces. Ruby didn't feel unsafe, but she didn't want to live like that, sticking out as the white girl. That seemed a few lifetimes ago. A lifetime when Ruby had felt sure of Ed and of what was between them.

Ruby found The Crone's building, a brownstone that had seen better decades and coincidentally resembled the one she and Ed had looked at in Bed-Stuy. The stoop's steps were chipped, and weeds were sprouting from holes where a railing had once been. There were three old-fashioned doorbells. None marked. Ruby couldn't decide which she wanted to do least, use the cell phone to call The Crone or ring all three doorbells and invoke ire from strangers. She opted for calling The Crone even though she thought it might give the woman a last-minute chance to back out.

The Crone grunted a hello, then grunted again when

Ruby told her she was downstairs. A few moments later, a boxy woman lumbered to the door.

"Hiya," she greeted Ruby.

"Hello, I'm Ruby." Ruby tried to sound sweet.

"So I gathered." The Crone emitted a short, sharp, barking sound that Ruby guessed was a laugh. "I'm Millie."

Millie was about Ruby's height, five-four, but considerably wider. Her dark, dense hair was cropped close to her head, her eyebrows were bushy, and she had no lips to speak of. Not that you'd want to speak of them if they'd been there. She was wearing a huge purple T-shirt over a pair of red sweatpants. The Crone's enormous breasts hung down to her waist.

"What can I do for ya, Ruby?" The Crone asked as she ushered Ruby into a dark, narrow hallway.

"I want to talk to you about Jody." Ruby followed The Crone up a set of stairs.

"Doesn't everyone," The Crone said.

"Really?"

"You and that fuckwad husband of hers. I guess that's why he sent you. He knew he wasn't getting nothin' out of me."

Ruby could hear Millie's breath coming in quick gasps. Even the modest effort of climbing the stairs was winding her.

"And don't tell Jody I used a double negative, will ya?"

Ruby laughed.

"She doesn't like me coming off like a moron," Millie said. "I always told her, if someone wants to pigeonhole me based on my using double negatives, that's their business. I'm not big on appearances."

They reached the top of the stairs where a door stood ajar. The Crone shuffled into the apartment ahead. The floors were lovely old wood parquet, and a chandelier hung from the ceiling. The walls were painted blood red, making the place seem vaguely threatening. Ruby followed The Crone into a living room crammed with droopy, expensive-looking furniture. Two old-fashioned French windows looked out over a large garden. The place was pretty but oppressive.

"Make yourself comfortable." The Crone motioned toward a red couch that matched the walls, then sat down in an armchair opposite Ruby.

"So Jody's on the lam?" The Crone said.

"Yeah. Tobias can't find her," Ruby said.

"What'd she do, take the kidnapping money and run?"

"Oh, so you know?"

"Sure. Jody tells me everything. Well, just about. She didn't tell me she was gonna take off with the money. But I could have predicted it. She looked like she was well on her way to an episode."

"Episode?"

"Fugue. Mental fugue. She gets a little lost sometimes. Little mini-breakdowns. She spirals and gets so low she can't move. Hard to say what brings it on, though in this case probably the husband pulling this stunt."

"Do you know where she might have gone?"

"Probably," said The Crone, slitting her eyes. "Remains to be seen if I tell you about it though."

"Ah," Ruby said. "What is it you do?" Ruby heard it pop

out of her mouth. Sometimes she wished she had a few seconds' warning before she found herself asking questions like this.

"Do?" The Crone looked peeved. "You mean what's an old white lesbian doing living in a really nice apartment in the heart of a black neighborhood?"

"Something like that," Ruby said, deciding she might actually like The Crone.

"I've done it all, darlin'," The Crone said. "Right now, I work for the CF Foundation. Cystic fibrosis. I had a kid sister died of it way back when. As for Harlem, my girlfriend's black. This is her place."

"Oh, I'm sorry," Ruby said, "about your sister I mean."

"It's okay. I'm over it," The Crone said.

Ruby smiled benignly and was about to ask The Crone if she had Jody's keys, when one of the most beautiful women Ruby had ever seen walked into the room. The woman moved fluidly, barely touching the ground. A pink cotton sundress exploded against her dark skin, and her black hair trailed in slender dreadlocks down her back. She came to perch on the arm of The Crone's chair and smiled a small, curious smile.

"Babe, this is Ruby, friend of Jody's. Ruby, this is Felicia, my wife," The Crone said.

Felicia's smile expanded, revealing a row of tiny, perfect teeth. She arched one eyebrow in Ruby's direction.

"Nice to meet you," Ruby said.

"How do you do?" Felicia said, coming over to Ruby to formally extend her hand.

Ruby shook the hand, taking a moment to marvel over exactly how stubby and white her own hand looked next to Felicia's. Ruby glanced over at The Crone's hands. They were tiny and puffy. She could almost imagine coarse black hairs sprouting from the palms.

"I'll leave you two to talk," Felicia said, turning and floating out of the room. She was presumably out of earshot when The Crone perked up. "How'd an old bag like me land a delicious piece of ass like that?" she asked, winking at Ruby. "I guess the gods like me," she shrugged and laughed, making herself jiggle.

Ruby laughed back and decided she really did like this Crone, who reminded Ruby of a forlorn young woman she'd had a lesbian encounter with in her early twenties. The woman, Matilda, had been exactly as physically attractive as The Crone. Which is to say, not at all. To this day Ruby, who didn't possess strong same-sex longings to begin with, had never figured out exactly what had possessed her to have sex with Matilda. But whatever it was, it probably went a long way in explaining how The Crone was doing very nicely for herself.

"So. You're a detective?" The Crone asked.

"No. I just agreed to look for Jody."

"What's wrong with that fucking Toby?" Millie burst out. "He never does anything right. No offense, little girl, but you don't look especially capable of going out to hunt someone's stray wife. Particularly not this stray wife."

"I can take care of myself," Ruby shrugged.

"I don't doubt that." The Crone winked so violently Ruby wondered if she had an eye disorder. "But you'll have to agree that Tobias should have hired someone who's actually in the business of finding people who don't want to be found."

"I just want to know if you can point me in the right direction," Ruby said, feeling very tired. "Tobias says you have keys to the brownstone. He'd like me to start by looking there."

"She's not there. I'm sure she's in Pennsylvania," The Crone said as if it ought to be obvious to anyone.

"Pennsylvania?"

"Trout Falls. She's got a little cabin there. I guess she never told the husband about it just in case she needed an escape. She's like that. Always keeping something secret. Part of why it didn't work out with me and her." The Crone's voice had grown distant, coming at Ruby from a couple of decades earlier. "Though part of it was the woman just likes cock too much to make it as a dyke."

Ruby winced.

"Sorry there, little girl." The Crone winked again. "Definitely more information than you needed. But yeah. Trout Falls. Even money she's there."

"Is there a phone number there? She's not answering her cell."

"She probably threw it in the river. And no, no phone down there that I know of. The woman hates phones."

"She does?"

"Sure does," The Crone said.

"Oh," Ruby said. She felt slightly cheated. She was pretty

sure she'd complained to Jody about her own hatred of telephones. But The Psychiatrist had never let on that she felt the same way. Of course, at this point it was clear that there was a whole lot Ruby didn't know about Jody Ray. Hatred of telephones was definitely the least of it.

The Crone fished through the drawer of a writing desk, found an address book, and gave Ruby the address of Jody's Trout Falls hideaway.

"Got no idea where in Pennsylvania the place is though, girl. You're on your own. And here," she added, producing a key ring from a pocket in her sweatpants, "here's the key to Jody's apartment. Be my guest—go on over. You ain't gonna find her there though."

"Thanks," Ruby said, a little surprised. She'd expected a little more fight from Millie before surrendering the information and the key.

"I'd love to chat with you all day," Millie said, "but I gotta go to work soon."

"Of course." Ruby got to her feet. "Thanks, Millie."

"I guess this will be one more reason for Jody to be pissed at me." Millie sighed. "I don't like that creepy husband one bit, but Jody's gotta stop running at some point. And she could be in trouble," The Crone said a little ominously. "You seem like a nice enough girl. Go find her. Make her face reality."

Ruby wanted to remind The Crone that, as Jody's patient, it wasn't really Ruby's job to make her psychiatrist face reality. Instead, she smiled.

"It was nice to meet you, toots," The Crone said. "Good luck with this."

"You too," Ruby said. "And thanks for all your help."

"Not a problem." The Crone winked one last time, then closed the door after Ruby.

Ruby went down the stairs two at a time. She needed air. Badly.

It was humid outside and low-slung gray clouds crowded the sky. Ruby stood at the top of the stoop for a few seconds, gulping in air, but there really wasn't anything to gulp. She felt woozy. She debated between a cigarette and a Fireball, decided on the latter, and fished one from her pocket. She popped the candy into her mouth and started walking toward her car. And then felt something. A little shiver down her back. She turned around and saw a black-haired man walking a few feet behind her. Ruby looked right at the guy and registered something intensely familiar. Not good familiar. She stopped in her tracks. The guy kept his eyes down as he walked right past her. Ruby watched him disappear around a corner. She slowly walked to her car. She looked left and right then unlocked the Mustang and got in.

It took her a good five minutes, but Ruby was finally pulling out of the parking spot when she heard a squealing sound and her car lurched unnaturally forward. Ruby's chest banged into the steering wheel, winding her. She gasped for air then looked into her rearview mirror, where she saw a blue Honda with a dark-haired man at the wheel. Ruby opened her door to get out, saw the Honda backing up, and realized it was going to try running her over. She jumped onto the sidewalk in time to see the Honda plow into the spot where she'd been standing, nicking her car door in the process.

"Hey, motherfucker!" some girl yelled on Ruby's behalf.

Ruby glanced at the license plate as the blue Honda sped away, but her eyesight wasn't the greatest and all she saw were the first two letters, BK.

"Did you see that shit?" A young woman, the one who'd called Ruby's attacker a motherfucker, had rushed over to Ruby's side. "That fucking guy was trying to hit you!"

Ruby was flooded with adrenaline. She collapsed onto the lip of the sidewalk, held her head between her hands for a moment, and took a few deep breaths.

"You okay?" The girl had come to sit next to Ruby.

She glanced at the tough-looking young girl. The girl was wearing a muscle-T showing skinny arms.

"Yeah, I'm all right," Ruby said. She put one hand to her breastbone. She still felt a little funny there, but not as though anything was broken or pierced.

"I'm calling the cops." The girl had fished a cell phone from her pocket and was dialing.

"Thanks," Ruby said.

As Ruby listened to the girl reporting the incident, she tried to make sense of what had happened.

"I'm Victoria," the girl said after she'd closed her phone.

"Ruby. Thanks for calling the cops." She shook Victoria's hand.

"They should get here sometime next week." Victoria smirked. "What was that all about? Someone trying to take you out?"

"It looked that way, didn't it?" Ruby said. "But I don't know why. I didn't realize anyone had it in for me."

"You piss off an ex-boyfriend or something?" Victoria asked. "I had one come after me in a car one time," she added without waiting for Ruby's answer. "Motherfucker didn't even know how to drive. Got his auntie's car and tried to run me down but hit a parked car instead. And all I'd done was tell him he wasn't getting no pussy no more."

"Some men don't take that well," Ruby said.

"No shit." Victoria shook her head. Her long silky dreadlocks moved.

Normally, Ruby thought dreadlocks looked stupid on white people. In spite of being blond, Victoria somehow pulled it off.

Victoria didn't seem to have anything better to do, and she hung around as Ruby inspected the Mustang. It had a serious dent but seemed structurally intact, as far as Ruby could tell.

The cops showed up after about fifteen minutes, by which time Ruby had heard most of Victoria's sexual history. And it wasn't pretty.

Ruby popped a Fireball, and one of the cops, a young Spanish guy with a spindly mustache, stared at Ruby's mouth as she sucked the candy. Ruby spit the Fireball out. Both she and the cop watched it roll away into the gutter.

It was a long half hour while Ruby answered the cops' questions and filled out forms. She knew she should mention that this wasn't the first time she'd seen the blue Honda, but she didn't. It would have led to too many additional questions she didn't want to answer. When the police were done with her, they left her there, alone with Victoria, who didn't seem to have anything better to do than hang around rubbernecking. Other passersby had come and gone, but Victoria hadn't found a reason to leave and was sitting on the sidewalk near Ruby's car.

"I guess I'm gonna get going," Ruby told her.

Victoria shrugged. "Yeah. Well. Watch yourself, girl."

"I will. Thanks for your help," Ruby said. "You need a ride somewhere?" Ruby added, not expecting to be taken up on it.

"I wouldn't mind," Victoria said. "I'm late for work."

"Oh." Ruby couldn't help expressing her surprise. "Where should I drop you?"

Victoria gave Ruby an address in the West Fifties. "I'm a stripper," she added.

This was basically the last occupation Ruby would have pegged on the skinny, flat-chested woman.

"Good money," Ruby said.

"You done it?"

"For about five minutes. I'm not much of an exhibitionist. I just felt naked."

Victoria laughed.

"Yeah. Well I like it," she said. "Gets me off taking those shit-heels' money."

They were in the car now, Ruby marveling over the fact that she was about to drive into the hideousness of Midtown traffic.

Victoria prattled on about men, stripping, and drinking,

apparently her three favorite topics. This successfully kept Ruby from worrying so much about traffic. In twenty minutes, she was dropping Victoria outside the strip club.

"You ever want to come in, just ask for me. I'll give you a free lap dance," Victoria said.

"Oh," Ruby said. "Thank you." She wasn't really sure how to interpret that one.

"My dancing name is Dazzle," Victoria added before shutting the Mustang's passenger door.

Ruby took a deep breath, then drove downtown.

Ruby circled Jody's block on Charles Street for twenty minutes before finally getting a parking spot. She was tired, her head was throbbing, and she felt right at the edge of hysterics. She closed her eyes, rubbed her eyelids, then got out and locked the car.

Jody's block was tree lined and packed with good-looking brownstones. It was very quiet, expensive quiet.

Ruby took out the keys The Crone had given her then tried two before getting the front door open. Jody occupied the two bottom floors, with a tenant at the top. Ruby entered through the garden-level door. The huge apartment was as beautiful as Ruby had expected. The ceilings were high, even on the lower floor. The dark wood floors were gorgeous; the furniture was tasteful and timeless. Even the carefully selected antique light fixtures were perfect. Ruby wanted to move in. To assume the lovely life that went with it. Only that life didn't appear to be quite as lovely as Ruby had once thought.

Ruby went into the bathroom, threw water on her face, and peed. She still felt horrible, and when her explorations of the apartment led her to the bedroom, she sprawled out on the immense bed. It was soft, very soft.

Ruby came to abruptly a half hour later. She'd been dreaming about Ed. He'd been walking down a busy street ahead of Ruby, not waiting for her. She kept trying to catch up with him but never did.

Ruby went into the bathroom again, splashed more water on her face, then started rooting through the apartment. There were immense closets filled with well-made clothes and shoes. There was a lovely kitchen, an expensive-looking stereo and TV and walls lined with hardcover books. Ruby couldn't find a computer though. She knew Jody had a laptop, had seen it at The Psychiatrist's office, so she assumed Jody had taken it with her. Ruby didn't find anything useful in the desk drawers in the study.

She went to sit in the dining room and put her face in her hands, trying to empty her mind. She was vaguely expecting some revelation, some sense of her psychiatrist, anything. But no. All she got was a headache and the idea to check with the tenant upstairs.

A tall, fortyish man with a mustache answered Ruby's knock.

"Yeah?" he scowled down at Ruby. He was wearing a black silk robe, and his long hair hung past his shoulders. He looked like a medieval king recently back from conquest.

"Hi. I'm trying to find Jody Ray," Ruby said simply.

"Well she ain't in here," he said as though Ruby had just accused him of harboring the fugitive psychiatrist.

"I was wondering if you'd seen her lately and if she said anything to you. I'm a friend of her husband's. She's missing."

"Oh," the guy said, softening. "You want to come in?"

Ruby had the feeling the guy might eat her for dinner. But maybe he knew something. "Sure, thanks," she said.

The apartment was similar to Jody's, though the ceilings weren't quite as high and the many windows were covered in heavy curtains. An enormous computer monitor sat on top of a mahogany desk. The screen was filled with dense, tiny strings of text.

"Code," the guy said, noticing that Ruby was looking. "I'm a programmer. Name's Paul, by the way."

Ruby told him her name and suddenly felt tongue-tied. Paul was standing a bit too close to her, making her nervous.

"When was the last time you saw Jody?" she asked.

"Sit down," Paul said, motioning to a dark green couch.

Ruby sat.

"About a week ago," Paul said. He was still standing and had folded his arms over his chest. He looked like a prosecutor about to go in for the kill.

"Saw her leaving the building when I was coming home. She was with some guy. Not the husband. Young guy. You don't expect me to believe you're a cop do you?"

"No," Ruby shook her head, "just a friend. Did Jody say anything when you saw her?"

"'Good morning' maybe. Some pleasantry like that. It's not like we were in the habit of having heart to hearts."

"What did the young guy look like?"

Paul frowned. "I don't know." He shrugged. "Maybe mid-twenties. Brown hair. Skinny. Shorter than me. The hair was kind of long. All one length."

Now it was Ruby's turn to frown. The description seemed familiar somehow. Even though she couldn't think of anyone fitting it.

"How did she act toward the guy?"

"I don't know. The guy was carrying stuff. Maybe suitcases. Yeah, that's right." Paul's face became animated. "I remember I wondered if he was some sort of hired help or if she was running off with him. I haven't seen the husband in a while."

"They're separated," Ruby said.

"Too bad," Paul said, though he didn't seem worked up about it. "How about you?"

"How about me what?"

"Are you separated?"

"What?"

"I mean are you single?"

"No, I'm not single," Ruby said more severely than she'd intended.

"No offense," Paul said. "Had to take a shot." He grinned.

"No offense taken," Ruby said. "And thanks for your help." She rose from the couch and made a beeline for the door.

"Hey, I didn't mean to scare you," Paul said.

"No, it's fine. I just have to go." She looked up at him. He was cute in a towering-ogre sort of way.

"Thanks for your help, Paul."

"Anytime," he said.

Ruby walked into the hall and down the steps two at a time. She got into her car and immediately lit a cigarette. It made her feel worse. She turned the radio on and played with the dial until she hit pay dirt, an Elliott Smith song, "Pictures of Me," on one of the college stations. Ruby loved the song, even though listening to Elliott Smith always made her angry at the guy for killing himself. When the song ended, Ruby moved the dial over to WKCR. Beethoven's cheerful, pathologically optimistic Sixth. Always a pleasure.

Ruby took her phone out of her pocket to make sure no one had called. No one had. Ruby called her bank's automated phone number, punched in her account number, and discovered that Tobias had kept his word. Ruby's balance was up by a thousand bucks.

Ruby nosed the car into traffic. She was putting Tobias and Jody on hold and going to Belmont to try talking to Ed again. She had to do it.

———

FORTY-FIVE MINUTES LATER, Ruby pulled her car into a spot at the end of Ed's shed row. She popped a Fireball in her mouth and got out of the car.

Nicky the groom was leading Bend Sinister, an older gray gelding, toward his stall. Nicky nodded at Ruby.

"Seen Ed?" she asked.

"Right there." Nicky pointed to Juan the Bullet's stall just as Ed emerged from it.

At first, Ed reacted naturally: He smiled. Then the smile froze, and he looked uncomfortable.

Ruby had thought words would come easily. Or that maybe that she wouldn't need words, that Ed would throw his arms around her and the whole unpleasant mess would be history.

Nicky was watching the whole interaction. Ruby wanted to tell him to take a hike.

"Can we talk?" Ruby asked Ed in a small voice.

He stared at her, opened and closed his mouth, then slowly shook his head.

"I can't. Not yet. Need more time." He looked down at his work boots.

"Please?"

"Can't do it. I'm sorry." He looked at her and, for a moment, was himself. Then he frowned. "Sorry," he said. He turned and walked away.

Ruby didn't have any fight left. She made a face at Nicky, who'd continued to stand there the whole time; then she walked away, making a beeline for Violet's barn.

It had rained during the night, and Ruby wasn't looking where she was going. She walked through a huge puddle, and her red sneakers got muddy. She didn't care.

Ruby found the door to Violet's office open. Henry was at the desk, bent over some paperwork.

"Can I come in?" Ruby asked.

"Huh?" Henry looked up, startled. It seemed to take him a few seconds to process who Ruby was and what she wanted.

"Violet's not in here," he said, though this was perfectly obvious.

"Could I wait for her?"

"Sure," Henry said. A vein in his temple started throbbing. "I was just leaving," he said, getting up from the desk.

"Please don't go," Ruby said.

"Really, I was leaving anyway," Henry said, barely meeting her eyes.

Ruby tried not to take it personally. Henry had the social skills of a parking meter, and Ruby knew he liked her as well as, if not more than, he liked most people. But that didn't translate into his feeling comfortable with her in a small space.

Ruby sat down on the couch, leaned her head back, and closed her eyes. She thought about The Crone and Victoria the stripper. She briefly imagined taking Jane with her to get a lap dance from Victoria. Jane had once dragged Ruby to a strip club when one of her yoga friends, a slender Finnish girl named Tanya, had been earning her keep getting naked for strangers. Though Tanya had invited Jane to come see the place, she seemed embarrassed to be seen there in her skimpy, shimmery outfit. Jane and Ruby hadn't stayed long.

"Are you all right?"

Ruby opened her eyes. She hadn't heard Violet come in.

"Sorry for the unexpected visit," Ruby said.

"I always expect you to visit."

Ruby smiled. "Thank you."

"You don't look well. Are you all right?"

"Ed still isn't speaking to me. And I took a job at a game in the amusement park."

Violet's eyes rounded in amazement, and suddenly Ruby didn't know why she hadn't called her friend all this time. But Ruby's instinct was to hide when things got bad, to crawl into a small dark area like a hurt animal.

"It's been horrible."

"Tell me," Violet said. She was sitting in her office chair, palms on her thighs, eyes round and earnest.

Ruby told her.

"And now I have to take a little road trip to Pennsylvania to look for Jody," Ruby said after she'd recounted most of it.

"Can't you call her?"

"Doesn't have a phone there."

"Cell?"

"I've been trying her cell. No good. She probably threw it in the river. At least, that's what The Crone said."

"The who?"

"Millicent. The woman I went to see this morning. Tobias calls her The Crone."

"Oh."

"She *was* sort of cronish, but nice enough. And she gave me the address of Jody's secret place in Pennsylvania."

"What secret place? Where in Pennsylvania?"

"Some tiny town. I haven't looked at the map yet," Ruby said.

Violet was on the verge of asking Ruby something else when Henry came into the office.

"I know I'm forgetting something," he told Violet.

"I'm sure you are." She smiled at Henry. "We have a filly running." Violet turned to Ruby. "Henry's latest folly is that whenever we've got one running, he becomes convinced he's forgotten something and wanders around like a ghost until post time." She said it affectionately, but Henry looked slightly hurt.

"I'm not being crazy, woman," he said, walking out of the office.

"Which filly is running?" Ruby asked.

"Half Mad. She'll be a long shot. But she's finally started showing a competitive streak in the morning. We're hoping she might do some running this afternoon."

Ruby nodded. Without hope and pathological optimism, horse racing wouldn't exist. It's one of the things that made Ruby love it in spite of having reservations over the fates of the sport's lesser known horses and humans.

"She'd better run well," Violet added. "Henry and I need something to go right after losing Fearless Jones."

"I know," Ruby said.

"Cretins," Violet said.

This was about as strong a word as Ruby had ever heard Violet use.

"I know you don't want to hear this, and probably won't believe it, but another good one will come along."

Violet didn't look convinced. She changed the subject. "One of my grooms has gone missing," she said.

"Oh?" Ruby tried to seem more interested than she actually was as Violet told her how her favorite groom, Elliott, had taken off, leaving a note of apology but no explanation.

"It's so unlike him. Elliott was always the most reliable of my boys."

Ruby liked the way Violet called the grooms and hotwalkers her "boys," even when some of them were women.

"Which one is Elliott?" Ruby asked.

"White. Young. Longish brown hair. Pretty eyes?" Violet was watching Ruby's face for signs of recognition.

Something clicked.

"Was he friendly with Jody?"

"Oh yes, very," Violet smiled. "All my owners liked him."

Ruby was thinking of Jody's tenant Paul and of his description of the young man he'd seen Jody with.

"Do you think he would have run away with Jody?"

"Run away with Jody? Of course not. What makes you ask such a question?"

Ruby told Violet about Paul's description of Jody's companion.

Violet's mouth opened half an inch. Then closed. Then opened again.

"Do you think . . . ?" She let the question hang.

Ruby nodded slightly.

"Elliott though? He's so sweet."

"Exactly."

"Is there something I don't know about Jody?" Violet asked. Her forehead was creased, and her eyes had gotten smaller.

"There's apparently a lot we don't know about her."

"Elliott's a good boy," Violet said defensively. "He did get kicked out of his girlfriend's a few weeks ago," she admitted. "I put him in the little cabin." She motioned toward the front of the barn, where there were two bungalows. Some trainers used these as offices; others housed their workers there.

"Can I look around?" Ruby asked.

"Oh, Ruby, I don't know. That would be a terrible breach of privacy."

"I thought you said he left a note that he wasn't coming back?"

"He didn't say he wasn't coming back. Just that he had to go off for a while. Some of his things are still in the cabin."

Henry appeared in the office doorway once more.

"Time to go," he told his wife.

"Oh." Violet glanced up at the Belmont Park wall clock that had been a fan giveaway a few summers earlier. "So it is." She looked from Ruby to Henry and back.

"I'll be right there, Henry," she said.

In the end, Violet did give Ruby the key to the bungalow door.

"Don't disturb anything," she said.

"I'll be very careful," Ruby said. "Where should I leave the key when I'm done?"

"You're not going to come watch Half Mad's race?" Violet looked aghast. "It's the finale on closing day, and we've got one running. You *have to* watch."

"You're right," Ruby said. "It was insane of me to think otherwise."

Ruby told Violet she'd find her at the rail in a half hour.

————

ELLIOTT'S TWO-ROOM bungalow was dark but tidy. The tiny kitchen area was clean, plastic plates neatly stacked to the side of the sink. The narrow bed was made. A pressed-wood dresser contained a few pairs of socks and some old jeans. There wasn't a desk or any place where Elliott might have left indications of his whereabouts. All Ruby could tell from standing inside the bleak little bungalow was that its inhabitant had led a spartan existence. A life he was probably willing to abandon without much deliberation.

Ruby locked the bungalow door behind her then walked the few yards back to the barn. She went to stand in front of the stall Fearless Jones had inhabited. The bedding had been removed, and the hook where his halter had hung was empty. Ruby remembered the day after Fearless Jones had broken his maiden and equaled a track record for five-and-a-half furlongs. Someone from the *Daily Racing Form* had stopped by to chat with Henry and Violet. When asked what it was like to have a horse with that much potential, Henry had answered: "I guess it's better than an empty stall."

BETTER THAN AN EMPTY STALL had been the headline for the little story in the *Form* the next day.

———

RUBY STOOD IN THE spectator area of the paddock watching Violet and Henry struggling to tack up Half Mad. She was an opinionated filly, and her opinion was that the paddock was filled with too many scary things. Henry had to lead her out of the stall and walk her in a few circles before she finally let him tighten the girth. When the paddock judge called "Riders up," Henry gave Aaron Gryder a leg up. The filly let out a small buck, nothing serious, just trying to establish that she was in charge. Gryder seemed completely unfazed.

As the horses headed to the track, Ruby walked into the grandstand and got in line to place a bet before going to meet Violet in her preferred spot at the rail.

As a stooped old man in the next line leered at Ruby, she glanced at the tote board and saw that Half Mad had climbed to 48–1. Ruby never bet races she hadn't studied beforehand, but 48–1 on a horse that might have a chance wasn't something to pass up. She snuck a few glances at the program the guy in front of her was holding. She noticed that the 8–5 morning-line favorite, Loudermilk, a gray who'd caught her eye in the paddock, was hovering at a generous 9–2 while Shake Rag, a horse Ruby had seen run a few weeks earlier, was at a decent 6–1. When Ruby reached the front of the line, she boxed Shake Rag, Loudermilk, and Half Mad in a two-dollar trifecta then put four dollars on Half Mad across the board. The betting clerk, a young girl with limp red hair, wished Ruby luck. Ruby always tried to curb any tendencies toward superstition, but she had noticed that her bets came in approximately 75 percent of the time when the teller wished her luck.

Ruby went to find Violet at the rail. Her friend was staring out at the track but looked calm, almost serene.

"There you are," Violet said as Ruby came to stand next to her.

Ruby handed Violet the key to Elliott's bungalow.

"I didn't find anything incriminating."

"Good," said Violet.

"I put four dollars across the board on your filly."

"Oh, I think she'll run second."

Ruby didn't ask Violet why she hadn't told her this earlier. Violet was prone to what could only be called genuine psychic moments. Ruby had been standing next to Violet once when, a few seconds before a race went off, Violet had calmly informed Ruby that a 93–1 shot was about to win. The horse had paid a hundred eighty-nine dollars to win. Not that it did Ruby any good.

The bell sounded, and Violet and Ruby watched Half Mad break alertly then find a spot at the rail. The race was a mile and a sixteenth, and Aaron Gryder was neither holding her back nor asking her to run. Both horse and rider seemed content with their position, at the rail with one horse, Shake Rag, ahead of them.

In its form, it was one of the least dramatic races Ruby had ever seen. Shake Rag stayed in the lead, Half Mad stayed right behind her, and, to Half Mad's right, Loudermilk and the favorite kept bobbing noses for third. At the wire, it looked to Ruby as if Loudermilk's nose got there first, but it seemed too improbable. The payout on her trifecta would be close to astronomical.

Ruby couldn't feel her extremities.

"Are you all right?"

Ruby realized Violet was talking to her.

"Who was third?"

"I don't know." Violet shrugged. "But Half Mad was second."

"Yes." Ruby stared at the tote board, waiting for the order

of finish to be posted. "I may have hit the trifecta," she said quietly.

"Oh?" Violet looked pleased. Then her face changed when she realized it was going to be a very substantial trifecta.

Ruby held her breath until Loudermilk's number flashed in the show spot. Ruby screamed. And screamed again when, after two interminable minutes, the payout was posted: $2,935.00. Definitely better than an empty stall.

"Well, dear girl, you'd better head to the IRS window. And I'd better go see about our filly."

"Did you bet her?" Ruby asked.

"No. I didn't realize she was going to run second until right before the race."

Violet didn't seem particularly upset over missing a twenty-six-dollar place payout on her own horse.

"I'll give you some of it," Ruby said, carefully extracting her betting slip from her wallet.

"You certainly will not," Violet said. "I assume full responsibility for not having faith in my own horse. And now, my dear, I must go." Violet pecked Ruby on the cheek.

Ruby went to the nearest IRS window to cash her bets. The teller, a middle-aged man with a wild waft of gray hair, inserted her ticket into his machine.

"Nice going," he told Ruby.

She filled out the paperwork, posed for the IRS photo, thanked the teller, and darted into the ladies' room to stuff her enormous wad of cash all the way down into her panties. Ruby didn't exactly look like a high roller, but she'd had a lucrative trifecta ticket pickpocketed from her back pocket at

Saratoga years earlier. It hadn't been this kind of lucrative, but still. She'd been hypervigilant with tickets and money ever since.

Ruby walked out to the parking lot, got into the car, popped another Fireball, then headed home. She was still morbidly alone, but at least she was rich.

14. TRIP

As Ruby stood in the hall unlocking her apartment, Elsie opened her own door and peered out. There were dark circles under her eyes, and her face was puffy.

"You okay?" Ruby asked.

"Sick," Elsie said minimally, as if speaking might make it worse.

"Do you need something?" Ruby asked.

"I'm out of my special tea," Elsie said, uncharacteristically forlorn.

"Where can I go to buy you some?" Ruby asked dutifully.

Elsie didn't say anything, but her eyes filled and enormous tears slid down her cheeks.

"What?" Ruby asked. "What is it? I'll go get your tea—it's no bother."

"It's not that," Elsie said between sobs. "It's the baby."

"What?" Ruby's stomach tightened. "What's wrong?"

"The baby's fine as far as I know. It's that I'll be a bad mother."

"Oh." Ruby released the breath she'd been holding. This she could deal with. "Come on in. I have to feed the cats." She ushered Elsie inside her own apartment and offered her a seat in the kitchen. As Ruby prepared meat for the cats and then brewed some cheap black tea, Elsie vented about impending motherhood, and Ruby made soothing noises.

After twenty minutes, without any input from Ruby, Elsie came around to realizing she probably would do fine once the little tyke came into the world.

"But this tea is disgusting." Elsie made a face. "Where'd you get that crap?"

"Key Food."

Elsie rolled her eyes.

"I have a favor to ask," Ruby said.

"Anything, baby," Elsie said.

"Can you feed my cats tomorrow and maybe the next day?"

"Where you going?" Elsie frowned.

Ruby told her about the road trip to Pennsylvania. "You've still got a copy of my key, right?"

"Yeah, but you know Pietro's gonna get all wound up if he hears you're out doing crazy shit again," Elsie said.

"I'm not doing crazy shit," Ruby said, exasperated.

"I know." Elsie reached over to pat Ruby's hand. "But that's not how Pietro sees it. He's very protective of you."

"Just tell him I've gone to my mom's or something. Don't tell him I'm up to no good," Ruby said.

"So you admit it!" Elsie was triumphant. "You *are* up to no good!"

"Elsie." Ruby sighed. "I am not up to no good. I lost my job for reasons I don't yet understand, and now I'm being paid to go find my missing psychiatrist. It's not no good. It's just what it is."

"Ah," Elsie said.

They heard footsteps in the hall, and Elsie cocked her head. "Pietro's home," she said. She slowly rose from her chair, kissed Ruby's cheek, then waddled out onto the landing to greet her husband.

Ruby shut her door. She turned the overhead light on in the living room, but it still seemed dark in the apartment. She went through the entire place turning on all the lights. Once it was as bright as it could be, Ruby went to sit in front of her laptop. She went online and MapQuested Jody's address in Trout Falls, Pennsylvania. Ruby loved maps. She preferred hard-copy maps, but MapQuest and Google Maps had their own bonuses in being able to zoom in or out in any direction. The road Jody lived on was five miles from the actual town of Trout Falls, and Trout Falls itself was already in the middle of nowhere. Ruby noodled around online a while longer, making sure there were motels in the area. It would be easier to drive down tonight with no traffic on the highways. She'd get a motel room then go find Jody in the morning.

Ruby had just closed the computer when the phone rang. She lunged for it, thrilled that someone was calling, not caring in the slightest who it might be.

"Hello. Tobias here."

"Oh. Hi."

"Not who you were hoping for?"

"I visited The Crone." Ruby cut to the chase.

"See what I mean?" Tobias said.

"See what you mean what?"

"She *is* a crone, isn't she?"

"Sort of. But she was nice."

Tobias grunted.

"She gave me keys to the brownstone, but I didn't find anything there. I talked to the tenant upstairs."

"And?"

Ruby didn't know if she should tell Tobias that Jody had been seen with a guy, very possibly Violet's groom. She decided not to.

"He hadn't seen her in a while."

"That's it?"

"The Crone thinks Jody's in Pennsylvania."

"Pennsylvania?"

Ruby told Tobias about Jody's cabin. She felt sorry for Tobias when she heard the surprise in his voice. She asked how he was feeling.

"I won't be able to water-ski," Tobias said.

"Water-ski?"

"Not that I ever *have* water-skied, but that's precisely my point. I'm a cripple now. So many doors have been shut."

Ruby made sympathetic noises even though she wasn't feeling entirely sympathetic.

"I'm going to go down there tonight," she said once she'd expressed enough empathy.

"Down where?"

"Pennsylvania. I don't like driving on highways. It's better at night when they're not crowded. So I'm going tonight. I'll find a motel once I get close, then go look for Jody's cabin in the morning."

"I'll cover your expenses of course."

"Good."

"I'm very appreciative of the efforts you're making."

"You're welcome," Ruby said.

"So." Tobias paused. "I'll call you tomorrow?"

"Fine," Ruby said, "but there's a chance my phone won't work down there."

"Oh, right."

"You sure you don't want to give me a number where I can reach you?"

"I'm sure. I'll just try you."

"As you like it," Ruby said.

Tobias thanked her then hung up.

Ruby went into the bedroom to organize some things for her trip. She had just unearthed a little-used overnight bag when she thought she heard a key in her front door.

She stopped moving and listened. She heard it again. Ruby tiptoed over to the door. Someone was in the hall with a hand over the peephole. Ruby frantically looked around for something she could use as a weapon. Ed's overflowing tool-box was pushed up against the far living-room wall, and Ruby was about to scramble for a hammer or screwdriver when she heard Ramirez shouting in the hall. Something clanged to the floor. Ruby looked through the peephole again. The hand was gone. Ruby opened the door in time to see Ramirez running down the stairs clad only in boxer shorts and an undershirt.

"Come here, motherfucker!" Ramirez was shouting. Ruby ran down the stairs after him. She reached the street in time to see a black-haired man get into a blue Honda. The car flew forward into traffic.

Ramirez ran out into the street then stood flapping his arms helplessly when he realized he couldn't catch the car.

"Let's go find a cop." Ramirez seemed to have forgotten he was wearing only boxers and his undershirt.

"What good will that do?" Ruby asked.

Ramirez frowned. He had no love for governing bodies and no reason to think what had happened was anything other than a random break-in attempt.

"Yeah," he shrugged, "I guess. How'd that asshole get in the building though?"

"I don't know," Ruby said. "But we have to go back in. You're not dressed."

Two young girls were walking by and illustrated Ruby's point by erupting in giggles at the sight of Ramirez.

"Oh." Ramirez looked down at himself. "Right."

"Come on." Ruby motioned for him to follow her back inside their building.

"Thanks for looking out for me." She touched Ramirez on the arm as they reached the top of the stairs.

"Yeah," he said. "Maybe you should file a report with the cops."

"I might," Ruby lied. "I gotta go though. I'm taking a trip tomorrow, and I have to get ready."

"Where to?" Ramirez asked.

"Going to see my mom," Ruby said. She guessed that once Ramirez told Elsie about what had happened, Elsie would spill out everything Ruby had told her. Elsie, thankfully, seemed to have gone to bed early.

Ruby wished Ramirez a good night then went into her

apartment and collapsed onto the couch. As the adrenaline left her body, she felt the deepest exhaustion she'd ever felt. Her eyes got heavy.

Ruby came to an hour later. She had fallen asleep curled into a tight ball, and now she had a crick in her neck. She stumbled into the bathroom to pee, then looked at her watch. It was only 10:30 P.M.

She brought the phone with her into the bedroom while she finished packing. She called Triple and got him to agree to do her barn work at The Hole for the next two days. She promised him cash. He said he'd accept it.

When Ruby put her overnight bag next to the front door, Stinky meandered over and looked from Ruby to the bag. In a moment, Lulu joined him and pretty soon Ed's cats appeared too. All four glaring at her accusatorily, like she was some sort of cat-abandoning slut from hell. Ruby had read in one of her animal books that if you made a mental picture of yourself coming home, the cats could see it and would be reassured that you were eventually coming back to feed and admire them. Ruby dutifully took a moment to picture herself coming back home. This didn't seem to convince the cats. They kept on glaring.

Ruby had left the Mustang on Surf Avenue, and two teenage girls were sitting on the hood. They gave Ruby the evil eye as she came close. She smiled, reached for her car keys, and unlocked the driver's-side door. The girls reluctantly slid off the hood.

Ruby got in and pulled ahead into traffic. She was waiting for the light to change at the corner of West Seventeenth and

Stillwell when she saw her boss, Bob, standing at the corner. Ruby pulled over and rolled her window down.

"Hi, Bob," she said.

Bob, who had evidently been daydreaming, looked startled.

"Hi," he said, friendly at first, then remembering.

"You still think I stole money?" Ruby asked.

Bob wouldn't look her in the eye. She was getting used to that these days.

"Bob, look me in the eye."

"Murphy, you've fucked me. I don't want to look at you," Bob said, though he did actually look at her.

"You *are* looking at me."

"Don't remind me," he said, a hint of teasing in his tone.

The tone gave Ruby hope. "I would never steal from you. I wouldn't steal from anybody. I don't do that shit."

"Yeah." Bob was looking away again. "Maybe so. I need a break though, Ruby."

"A break?"

"I've got some stuff going on," he said, uncharacteristically vague. "I just need a break from strife."

"Oh," she said.

"Sorry," said Bob.

Ruby shrugged, wished Bob a good night, rolled up her window, and pulled back into traffic. She felt like shit.

15. SPIKE

Going close to 70 miles per hour on the New Jersey Turnpike was a rush for a while. Then the whole thing got creepy. There weren't any blue Hondas in sight, but it was after midnight and Ruby felt alone and defenseless. She drove a little faster.

From the New Jersey Turnpike, Ruby took the Pennsylvania Turnpike to 202 South. By the time she got onto 30 West, the road that would lead her into Trout Falls, Ruby started having trouble keeping her eyes open.

She had just decided to look for a motel when she saw a neon motel sign on her right and pulled in. The place was called, comfortingly enough, Comfort Pines Motor Lodge. It was a one-story horseshoe-shaped structure built around a small swimming pool that hadn't seen anything but dirty rainwater in a few years. Ruby pulled up near the office. A thin old man was asleep behind a pressed-wood desk. There were papers and fast-food containers everywhere, and the old guy was slumped over to one side, his head lolling at what looked like a painful angle. Ruby cleared her throat. The sound didn't wake him.

"Hi," Ruby said loudly.

The man nearly fell out of his chair. He scrambled to his feet and stared at Ruby with his mouth half open.

"What is it?" he asked as if expecting incredibly bad news.

"Could I get a room?" Ruby ventured.

"A room?" The man seemed incredulous.

"Yes. For one night."

"That's forty-nine ninety-nine," the man threatened.

"Do you take Visa?" Ruby asked, pulling out her credit card.

"Yeah," the man said, eyeing the card as if he expected it to be declined.

Ruby wondered if she looked that disreputable. More likely she had the aura of a city dweller, and in a lot of people's minds, living in cities indicated criminal inclinations.

After running Ruby's card through the machine, the old man turned around to gaze at the room keys dangling from hooks on the peeling green wall. He eyeballed Ruby once more before settling on the key to room number seven.

"You're not Joe Murphy's wife are you?" the man asked.

"Not that I know of, no." Ruby couldn't resist having a little fun.

"What's that supposed to mean?" the old guy barked.

"I don't know any Joe Murphy, and I'm not married," Ruby said.

This seemed to placate the old geezer.

"Checkout's at eleven," he told her.

"I'll be out long before then," Ruby promised, noticing flecks of spittle near the man's thin, bluish lips. "Have a lovely night," she added.

Ruby drove over to the parking spot in front of room seven, locked the car, and walked the few steps to her room. She was about to fit her key in the door when she saw a caramel-colored dog lying in the grass a few feet from her room door. When Ruby looked at him, the dog looked her right in the eye and started thumping his tail. He was a puppy with feet nearly as big as the rest of him. Ruby squatted down and extended one hand, palm up. The puppy ran over, licked her hand, and started wiggling so violently Ruby thought he might break. It was a he. No more than a few months old, maybe thirty pounds, with a black muzzle and a flashy splash of white on his chest.

"Hello," Ruby said, smiling at the dog. She remembered reading that dogs had been domesticated so long they understood human body language better than humans did. The puppy interpreted Ruby's smile as a good thing and tried to lick her face.

Ruby looked around, expecting to see the puppy's people somewhere, but there wasn't a soul in sight, nor were any lights showing in the windows of the other rooms. Ruby didn't know what to do, so she opened the door to her room. The puppy rushed in and jumped onto the bed. She sat down next to him and let him lick her cheek. She realized that she was one step away from taking the puppy home with her to Brooklyn and that she should make sure the dog didn't belong to some forlorn child who was home weeping her eyes out.

"Make yourself at home. I'm going to make inquiries," Ruby told the young dog. He tilted his head and wrinkled his brow.

As Ruby walked to the door, the puppy jumped off the bed and followed her.

"Stay here. I'll be right back," she said. The puppy had glued himself to her though, and when she opened the door, he went out. Ruby scooped him into her arms and held him as she walked to the motel office.

The old man was asleep again. Feet propped up on the desk. Ruby stood there, with the puppy in her arms, staring down at the old geezer. She was tempted to play some sort of prank on him. Tie his shoelaces together, put his hand in a bucket of hot water, something. The old guy must have felt her mischief. He opened his eyes and sat up.

"Huh?" He started blinking wildly.

"Whose puppy is this?" Ruby asked.

She watched the old guy fumble for a pair of bifocals.

"What do you want?" he asked.

"This puppy was in your parking lot."

"So?"

"You know this puppy?" Ruby looked down at the dog in her arms. He licked her chin. He was getting heavy, and Ruby rearranged him in her arms.

"That's Spike," the old man said, as if it were obvious.

"He's yours?" Ruby asked, resolving to rescue Spike from a life where he was left to his own devices in a parking lot at night.

"Ain't nobody's. Just turned up here a few weeks back. I feed him. Figure he'll be a good guard dog."

Unless he was going to ward off marauders by wagging his

tail and licking their hands, Spike wouldn't make much of a guard dog.

"I need a dog," Ruby announced. She figured it was going to cost her, but she didn't care. The old guy stared at her without saying anything, then shrugged.

"Well, you got one," he said.

Ruby was ready for an argument and was stunned not to get one.

"Seems to like you," the old man shrugged, "and I don't guess he'd make such a good guard dog, what with licking people like he does."

Ruby saw a flicker of tenderness come into the old man. It was as touching as it was unexpected. The old man got to his feet, opened a gray steel cabinet, and pulled out a bag of kibble.

"Here." He proffered the bag. "He'll be wanting breakfast in the morning."

Ruby put Spike down on the floor and took the bag.

"Thank you," she said, still waiting for the other shoe to drop.

"What are you gonna name him?" the old man asked.

"Nothing wrong with Spike," Ruby said.

The old man beamed. "He's gonna be a big one, you know," the old guy said, reaching down and grabbing one of Spike's paws. "Hundred pounds or so. Looks like he's got some Rhodesian ridgeback in him and maybe some Great Dane too."

Ruby nodded. Spike looked nothing like a Great Dane, but the last thing she wanted was to argue with the old guy.

"Well." Ruby wanted to get back to her room before the

old man reverted to his earlier crankiness. "Good night," she said, turning and walking out of the office.

Spike happily trotted next to Ruby, and when she opened the door, he jumped onto the bed and curled into a ball. Ruby had no idea if Spike was house-trained but figured she'd find out soon enough.

She stripped off her clothing and got under the covers without even brushing her teeth. She looked at Spike one more time before closing her eyes. He lifted his head and thumped his tail. She closed her eyes and fell into a dreamless sleep.

16. SHOT

It took Ruby a few minutes to remember where she was and why there was a dog in the bed. She stumbled into the bathroom to pee, and Spike followed, tilting his head, trying to figure out what she was doing.

Ruby brushed her teeth, threw water on her face, and let Spike out onto the grassy area in front of her room. The pup spun around in a few tight circles and immediately took care of business.

Ten minutes later, Ruby had repacked her overnight bag and was ready to go. She put Spike in the backseat of the Mustang, but as soon as she pulled out of the parking space, the dog scrambled into the front and settled into the passenger seat, maintaining eye contact with Ruby as he did, making a statement.

"Okay, fair enough," Ruby said.

Spike tilted his head.

Ruby made a right out of the motel driveway, heading for the town of Trout Falls, where she hoped to find a diner. She needed coffee, and Spike needed food since she wasn't about to feed him the by-product-infested kibble the old man had given her.

Main Street, Trout Falls, was lined with wood-frame houses

that looked as though they'd been built in the 1940s. Humble houses with plastic furniture and swing sets on front lawns. The town consisted of a decrepit five-and-dime, a gas station, a police station, and The Main Diner, a 1950s-looking silver diner. The parking lot was almost full. Either the place was good or, more likely, it was the only diner in town.

Spike tried to jump out when Ruby opened the car door, but she gently pushed him back and told him to stay. She wasn't sure he understood the specific command, but he got the general idea and settled back into the passenger seat after giving her a wounded look.

Either Ruby looked like shit, or Trout Falls was such a small town that residents weren't used to strangers coming into the diner. Everyone stared. As much as she sometimes loathed New York, Ruby liked the anonymity it conferred. This small-town stuff was nerve-racking.

She walked up to the counter to put in an order to go.

"What do you need, sugar?" asked a wrinkly peroxide-blond waitress who looked like a cigarette.

Ruby liked that the woman called her "sugar."

"Large coffee, scrambled eggs on a roll, and two burgers very rare with no buns."

"Coming right up, doll," the waitress said, as if perfectly used to people ordering two rare burgers with their morning egg sandwich.

Ruby settled onto one of the stools at the counter. To her left was a big man in a John Deere cap hunched over a plate of sausage and eggs. He didn't look at her, but Ruby sensed that he was aware of her. To Ruby's right was a small man nervously pushing his eggs around on his plate. He was also wearing a John Deere cap, the brim of which was pulled down to his nose, making Ruby wonder how he could see the cup of coffee in front of him.

"Food's ready, sugar," the waitress said after a short wait.

"Where's the nearest pet store?" Ruby asked the waitress when she handed Ruby her order. "I need to get my dog a collar."

"What kind of dog?" the waitress asked, getting that beatific animal-lover look on her face.

"Puppy. Mutt probably. Rhodesian ridgeback looking."

"You mean Spike from the motel?"

"Yeah," Ruby said, astonished.

"I tried getting that old grouch to give the dog to my niece, but he wouldn't. Musta liked you."

"Really?" Ruby was incredulous. If the old guy's treatment of her was from liking, she hated to think how he acted when he *dis*liked someone.

"You got a nice face, sugar. I'm sure people like you," said the waitress.

Ruby smiled. She'd beg to differ, but she didn't want to be rude.

"There's a Pet Mart about a mile down the road, little strip mall there. You can get everything you need. Here you go." She handed Ruby her bag of food. "Pay at the counter."

Ruby went to the counter and, as the cashier rang up her bill, helped herself to some after-dinner mints from the big bowl next to the cash register.

"Have a nice day," the cashier said.

Ruby went back to the car, broke the burgers into small pieces, and fed Spike in the take-out container. The puppy ate the burger bits in four mouthfuls then looked at Ruby as though he was ready for seconds.

"Later," said Ruby. Spike spun around in a circle then plopped down in the passenger seat.

Ruby made a right onto Main Street and, after a mile, found the pet store. She carried Spike in with her since she didn't want him trotting loose through the parking lot.

"Cute!" exclaimed a girl at the counter inside. She was a tiny Goth-looking girl with dyed black hair. Ruby hadn't realized Goth girls existed in places like Trout Falls.

The Goth girl, who immediately told Ruby she was a vegan and didn't believe in leather dog collars, helped Ruby select an attractive red nylon collar with a matching lead.

"You live around here?" the girl asked as Ruby paid for her purchases.

"No, just visiting."

"Why?"

Ruby laughed. "It's pretty around here."

The girl wrinkled her nose.

After putting Spike's new lead and collar on, Ruby walked the dog around the grassy fringe of the pet store parking lot. He sniffed a lot and peed a little before jumping back into the car.

Ruby pored over her various MapQuest printouts, running her finger along the route to Jody's house. Her stomach was in knots at the prospect of finding and confronting The Psychiatrist. Ruby had spent most of her life avoiding confrontations. She'd almost never fought with her parents, sister, or lovers. If there was friction, Ruby left. Even as a small child, when Ruby's parents had been upset with her or tried to make her do something she didn't want to do, she'd disappear, losing herself in the streets of Sunset Park as early as age five. Ruby's flight response had become a sore point with Ed. Rather than telling him when something was bothering her, she'd clam up or, in extreme situations, leave the apartment without a word. Ed hated this. Ruby had been trying to reform her ways— until Ed flipped out and started needing *space,* that is.

Ruby steered the Mustang out of the parking lot. Another five miles and she'd be looking for Maddox Road, where Jody's cabin was. Along the sides of the road, frame houses gave way to meadows and woods. There were fenced-in pastures where horses and cattle grazed.

The meadows hugging the sides of the road surrendered to dense trees, and Ruby slowed down. She found Maddox Road on her left and made the turn. It was a narrow two-lane road badly in need of paving. The trees grew denser and the sky was nearly shut out. The road rolled up and down several hills before Ruby saw what she hoped was Jody's driveway on her right. There weren't names or numbers on either of the mailboxes, but Ruby had gone the one point six miles Map-Quest wanted her to go. She slowly nosed the Mustang up the unpaved driveway. Spike started looking all around, sensing that they were arriving somewhere. After half a mile, Ruby saw a bright blue house on the left. An enormous woman in a pink housedress was sitting in a rocker on the front porch.

Ruby stopped the car and leaned out the window.

"Hi, I'm looking for Jody?" Ruby tried to sound cheerful.

The woman fanned herself with a magazine and squinted at Ruby. "She ain't here," she said.

"This is her house though?" Ruby asked, wondering if the large woman was a patient that Jody had, for mysterious reasons, brought along for the ride.

"Nah, next one down. Little white house. Like I said though, she ain't there. Saw her and that boy driving out a few nights ago, and they ain't been back."

"I guess I'll go on over to her house just to check."

"I may be fat, but I ain't blind," the woman said. "Jody ain't there."

"Thanks," Ruby said. "I just want to see the house. Maybe leave her a note."

The woman shrugged and rested her head on the back of her chair.

Ruby drove forward and, about a hundred yards down the road, came to the little white house. She got out, and Spike bounded out of the car and raced ahead into the shrubs surrounding the house.

"Spike!" Ruby panicked, imagining the dog disappearing into the forest and getting devoured by bears.

Spike emerged from the bushes, shook himself off, and looked at Ruby as though she was insane.

"Don't run off like that," she said. He tilted his head. "Stop being cute," she added.

Ruby knocked at the front door, softly at first, then adding a little force to it. Jody might have come back without the large neighbor's noticing. No one answered though. Ruby peered in the windows. There was a small kitchen with quaint 1950s appliances. The counters and sink were crammed with dishes.

Ruby tried the doorknob. It was locked but flimsy. She took out her bank card and did the honors. Utterly effortless. Spike trotted ahead into the little house. The garbage container was overflowing with empty cans, eggshells, and Styrofoam containers congealed with meat. Ruby had always thought of Jody as a tidy individual yet here she was breeding varmints in her kitchen. Ruby walked from the kitchen into the living room, calling out "Hello?" Nothing.

The mess was nauseating, and Ruby was starting to think her psychiatrist couldn't possibly live here when she noticed the elegant yellow purse on the kitchen table. Ruby had seen this purse a dozen times. She'd always admired its modishness even though she would have felt like a drag queen carrying such a purse. She contemplated the sacrilegious-seeming act of looking inside the purse and was about to open the clasp when she heard Spike knock something over in the living room. She went to see what the dog had gotten into. Clothes, luggage, and take-out containers were strewn all over the floor, and Spike was gnawing on the remains of a rotted roast chicken.

"You can't have that." Ruby tentatively tugged on the chicken. She didn't know if Spike had any food aggression. He let go without growling and stared at Ruby sadly as she put the rancid carcass into the kitchen garbage can.

Ruby went back to the living room. There were two crusted dinner plates on the wood table. An empty beer bottle. A full ashtray. Socks. It didn't quite make sense. She remembered Jody's apartment being spare and clean. Maybe Jody was completely unraveling, and a latent filthy streak was revealing itself after years of suppression.

There was a narrow wooden staircase at the far end of the living room, and Ruby climbed up to the second floor. There was a bathroom at the top of the stairs, and the rest of the floor was one open room serving as a bedroom. There were snarled bedsheets, two half-empty coffee mugs, a pair of red panties.

As Ruby went into the bathroom to explore the medicine cabinet, Spike came running up the stairs. The puppy rushed over to Ruby then started licking her hands and wiggling furiously, as if he hadn't seen her in years. Ruby laughed. Decided she might have completely lost her mind by now if it weren't for the dog. It hadn't even been a full day, and already she felt she couldn't live without him.

The medicine cabinet held only a bottle of ibuprofen and an ancient-looking dental floss dispenser. The strangest thing in the bathroom was the shower curtain. A clear plastic number with little pockets containing translucent plastic fish. Ruby never would have thought Jody whimsical enough to buy a fish-motif shower curtain. Frivolous household items were the sort of thing she and Jody had occasionally discussed during lulls in sessions when Jody had urged Ruby to speak— to say *Whatever comes to mind, Ruby*—and Ruby had volunteered some triviality, like having bought vivid pink flannel bedsheets on sale at Bloomingdale's. Never in the course of these mundane chats had Jody Ray admitted to a penchant for whimsical shower curtains.

Spike trotted after Ruby as she headed back down the stairs and into the kitchen. She picked Jody's yellow purse up off the table and opened it. Nothing but a packet of Kleenex. She turned the purse upside down, spilling out dimes, pennies, and half a roll of cherry LifeSavers.

Ruby sat down at the kitchen table. There was a Home Depot receipt inside an empty fruit bowl. Someone had bought plants and gardening tools. Ruby hadn't thought to look at the garden.

She didn't want to lose Spike in the shrubbery again, so she left him in the house while she went to poke around outside. She walked to the back, where a little garden area was fenced off against deer. A shovel was wedged into the ground. Ruby stared at the tomato plants, trying to envision her elegant psychiatrist digging around in the dirt. It didn't add up.

Ruby walked back around the side of the house and to the front. A blue car was parked next to the Mustang, and Ruby's heart did a few somersaults before she realized that it was not the Honda and that the large neighbor from down the road was standing at the front door.

"Hiya," said the woman. "Just seeing what you're up to here." She was narrowing her eyes at Ruby.

"Door was open. I'm just looking around," Ruby said.

The large woman obviously didn't believe her.

"Do you want to come in?" Ruby asked.

"You're inviting me in? Ain't even your house."

"That's true. But I have a right to be here."

"How's that?"

"Jody's husband asked me to come look for her. He couldn't come look for her himself. He's sick," Ruby said.

"And he couldn't just call her?"

"They had a little fight. She wouldn't answer his calls."

"Huh," said the woman. "And you're a friend of the family?"

"Yes. Why don't you come in," Ruby reiterated her offer. She wanted the woman to see that she wasn't up to anything nefarious.

The woman grunted and followed her inside.

Spike was at the door, wiggling. He tried to lick the big woman's hands, but she squealed and moved out of the way a whole lot faster than Ruby would have guessed she could move.

"He doesn't bite," Ruby said.

"I don't like dog drool," said the woman. She was standing in the archway between the kitchen and the living room, wiping her wet hand on her dress.

Ruby was offended on Spike's behalf. She picked him up so he wouldn't further violate the big woman.

"You don't think Jody's dead, do you?" the woman asked out of the blue. She was still standing under the archway, still wiping her hand on her dress.

"What?"

"She didn't look good the other day. She sick or something?"

"No, of course not."

"Okay," the woman shrugged, "I'm just trying to help."

Ruby said nothing. Spike was already getting heavy, so she put him down. He instantly trotted over to the big woman, sat, and stared up at her.

"My husband looked kind of funny and gray about a week before he dropped dead," the woman said, ignoring Spike. "Name's Dolly, by the way." She suddenly seemed to warm to Ruby. She took a few steps toward her and extended her hand.

"Ruby," said Ruby, shaking the hand. Ruby hated people with weak handshakes, and her estimation of Jody's large neighbor improved when Dolly gripped Ruby's hand firmly.

"Jody looked ill?"

"I dunno really. I'm just saying she was kinda gray looking same as Gil, my husband. Turned out he had a big ol' clot in his brain. One night he's lying on the couch eating chips and watching TV. I go into the kitchen to get some juice. I come back. Boom, he's dead. I knew right away he was dead. Just one look at him. Death is funny that way—how you know it right off."

"Uh huh," said Ruby. She hadn't seen many dead people, but she did agree that dead people looked dead. No doubt about that.

"You know," Dolly said after a pause, "I think Jody's prob-ably at Delaware Park."

"Delaware Park? Why?" Ruby asked.

"That's what they were saying. Her and the boy she had with her," Dolly shrugged, making her chest jiggle. "I guess the boy had a lead about a job at the track there. They were asking me for directions. I've been known to go to the races, you know." Dolly lowered her voice and looked over her shoulder, as if upholders of the community standard might be lurking there, waiting to incriminate Dolly as a filthy horse-player.

"But wouldn't they have come back? What, they're just going to go to Delaware Park and stay there? What's Jody going to do?"

"I don't know about none of that," Dolly said. "All's I know is they asked me about how to get there. Then, next thing I know, they're driving off and ain't been back since. Look, I'm enjoying chatting with you, but I gotta put my feet up. I got bad varicose veins. Ten minutes standing up and I'm in pain."

Ruby watched Dolly, who seemed familiar with the lay-out of Jody's house, go into the living room, sink into an arm-chair, and make herself comfortable propping her legs on an ottoman.

"I'm sorry," Ruby offered, not knowing what else one said under such circumstances.

"Ain't your fault. It's genetic. My pop had 'em too. Plus I'm fat. That don't help."

Ruby didn't know what to say to that either, so she offered Dolly a glass of water. Dolly declined.

"Just give me a minute and I'll be good as new," Dolly said.

Ruby had no reason to hang around Jody's any longer, but she didn't want to rush Dolly. She sat down on the couch op-posite Dolly and arranged Spike in her lap. He'd probably be too big for anyone's lap in another few weeks, but for now it was nice having him there.

Ruby glanced up at the wall clock and saw that it was just after 10 A.M. Outside, clouds had drifted over the sun and the day had turned dark.

17. STALKED

Before Ruby could come up with something to talk to Dolly about, the big woman started snoring. Ruby stared at Dolly in disbelief and wondered if maybe the woman was narcoleptic. She thought of the Gus Van Sant movie where the late River Phoenix played a narcoleptic male hustler. She tried remembering how River Phoenix had died in real life but couldn't. She moved on to thinking about River's brother Joaquin Phoenix in the movie *Gladiator.* Which led her to thinking of *Gladiator* director Ridley Scott, who had made one of Ruby's favorite movies, *Blade Runner.* She managed to thoroughly distract herself until her cell phone started ringing in her back pocket. She maneuvered to get the phone out without disturbing Spike in her lap.

"Yes," she said.

"Hello," Tobias said.

He'd gotten presumptuous enough to assume that Ruby would know his voice.

"Who's this?" Ruby asked, to irritate him.

"Tobias," he said impatiently.

Ruby gently pushed Spike off her lap then got up to walk outside for some privacy even though Dolly hadn't stirred.

"Still no sign of your wife," Ruby said, closing Jody's front door behind her. She wasn't in the mood for small talk. "I'm at her house right now."

"What's it like?"

"It's a mess. There's a neighbor who thinks maybe Jody went to Delaware Park."

"The track?"

"Yeah."

"Alone?"

"Doesn't sound like it."

"Oh," said Tobias.

"You're still not going to tell me where you are?"

"Why should I?"

"So I could call you with updates."

"Our current system is working for me just fine."

"Ah."

"I'm sorry if this is a burden to you."

"It's okay. I agreed to it."

"Yes. You did. Well," Tobias paused, "I'll check in with you later?"

"Sure," Ruby said.

He hung up. Ruby closed her phone. She went back inside and found both Spike and Dolly standing in the kitchen.

"Where'd you go?" Dolly asked, speaking for both of them.

"Had to take a call. Didn't want to disturb you."

"Uh," Dolly grunted. "You gonna keep hangin' around here or what?" She put her hands on her hips.

"I guess I'll go to Delaware Park. Try my luck there."

"Uh," Dolly grunted again.

"How far is it from here?" Ruby asked. She had a vague

idea that Delaware abutted Pennsylvania at some point, but she didn't know where.

"About an hour. You got a map?"

"Yeah," Ruby nodded, "in the car. Wanna show me?"

"Sure," Dolly shrugged. She looked around the place one last time then walked outside.

Ruby locked the doorknob lock then pulled the door shut behind her. She got her MapQuest printouts out of the car and spread them on the hood.

"What's this?" Dolly frowned so hard her eyebrows became one.

"MapQuest."

"Uh. Well. Delaware Park ain't on here."

"I know. Just show me the right direction."

Dolly did as Ruby asked.

"Well," Ruby said when she'd made a few notes.

"You want some chicken for that dog?" Dolly asked out of the blue.

"What?" Ruby wasn't sure she'd heard right.

"Chicken. I got some spare chicken. You want some for the dog for the road?"

"Uh, sure, yes, thank you," Ruby said.

"Meet me at my house," Dolly said. She opened her car door and slowly lowered herself onto the seat.

Ruby put Spike in the Mustang then got in.

It took Dolly a few tries to get out of her car, and Ruby felt bad for her. Dolly had started reminding Ruby of Stinky, who was overweight for mysterious reasons. For the most part, the big cat got along fine, even seemed proud of his size, but sometimes he struggled to jump up onto things, and he always looked horribly embarrassed by any lack of grace he might exhibit.

Ruby left Spike in the Mustang and followed Dolly up onto her porch.

"Wait here," Dolly said.

Ruby waited, wondering if Dolly had something in there she didn't want Ruby to see or if she was just a keenly private person.

After a few minutes, Dolly came back out onto the porch. She was puffing as though she'd just climbed Everest.

"Here you go." Dolly handed Ruby a big hunk of chicken wrapped in plastic.

"This is great," Ruby said. "Thank you, Dolly."

"No problem," the large woman said.

"Would you mind calling me if you see Jody come back?" Ruby had written her cell phone number on a sheet of paper from a small notebook in her glove compartment.

"I got a feeling she ain't coming back," Dolly said.

"Why?"

"Just a feeling I got."

"You mean she's gonna sell her house?"

"No," Dolly frowned. "Just not coming back."

It sounded so ominous that Ruby left it alone.

"Take care, and thank you," Ruby said.

"You too," said Dolly. She looked sad. She had been so gruff with Ruby for the first half hour of their acquaintance-ship, but now that Ruby was leaving, Dolly seemed melancholy.

Ruby tried to come up with something soothing to say,

could think of nothing, and got back into her car. Spike jumped into her lap and licked her chin. Ruby gently pushed the dog back to his side then drove to the end of the long driveway before stopping the car to gather her thoughts. She longed to go home and crawl under the covers. Eat Cheerios in bed. Wallow. But Delaware Park wasn't that far away, and she might be able to find Jody within a few hours.

Ruby lit a Marlboro then called Violet to see if her friend could put her in touch with Ann Julian, a trainer they both knew at Delaware Park. Violet answered on the eighth ring, sounding harried.

"What do you need to do at Delaware Park?" she asked after Ruby had told her that she wanted to get in touch with Ann Julian.

"I think Jody's there. At least, that's what her neighbor told me."

"And are you keeping yourself safe in all this?"

"Yes."

"Why don't I believe you?"

"I'm not sure."

"Please, be careful, yes?"

"I will, Violet."

Ruby closed her phone and drove forward.

The clouds above had thinned, and the day had turned beautiful again.

———

SOON AFTER RUBY passed back through Trout Falls, she felt her spine tingle. She glanced at her rearview mirror and nearly vomited. The blue Honda was there. *Right* there, practically tailgating her. She could make out the driver's black hair. The face was a little indistinct, but it gave her that creepy frisson of recognition all the same. Ruby memorized the New York plate. Then, seeing a driveway off the road on the left, she made a sharp turn into the driveway, turned around, and gunned the Mustang back to the police station in Trout Falls. She pulled up in front and got Spike out of the car in case her stalker tried to break in. She marched to the front door of the 1970s-looking structure.

"Can I help you, miss?" A man in a police uniform greeted her at the door.

"I need to file a complaint. Someone's stalking me."

The cop looked a little bewildered. He scratched his head. "You live around here?"

"No, just passing through town. But this individual's following me in his car."

"This a boyfriend that's following you?"

"No," Ruby said, irritated. "I don't know who it is."

"Oh," the cop said, looking even more confused. He was a pleasant enough looking guy in his early fifties, on the shorter side of the spectrum, with a mop of curly black hair and small wire-rimmed glasses. He looked more like a demented surgeon than a sheriff, which is what he turned out to be.

"This man has been stalking me for a while," Ruby said.

The sheriff's eyes got big, and he turned back to look at a female cop sitting at a desk.

Ruby wondered if they thought she was insane.

"I'm not making this up," she said, realizing that her saying this made it sound as though she *was* making it up.

"No one said you were, miss." The female cop rose from the desk. As she stood up, Ruby saw that the cop was very pregnant. Ruby thought of the movie *Fargo*. Frances McDormand in *Fargo* was the only pregnant cop Ruby had ever seen. You sure didn't see them on the streets of New York, even in tame, post-Giuliani New York.

"Thank you," Ruby said.

"Cute dog," the pregnant cop said.

"Thank you," Ruby said again. It was all so pleasant.

"Come on," the sheriff motioned for Ruby to follow him, "let's get some facts." He led her into a small, cluttered office. There were cheerful wildlife posters on the walls and stacks of books everywhere.

"It started a few weeks ago," Ruby said, settling into the chair the sheriff had offered. She didn't want to push her luck by putting Spike in her lap, so she made a "down" motion with her hand a few times, and on her third try, the pup crouched down and rested his head on his paws.

Ruby launched into all the facts about the blue Honda. She gave the sheriff the plate number she'd memorized, and he called out to the pregnant cop to have her run the plate. Ruby told the sheriff how the Honda's driver had tried to run her down in Harlem. Sheriff Jaffe, who interrupted Ruby's discourse to introduce himself at one point, was displeased with Ruby for failing to tell the New York cops about her stalker.

"I know. It was just stupid," Ruby said, hanging her head and trying to look contrite enough to arouse sympathy.

"Not a whole lot I can do for you at this stage," the sheriff said.

"That sounds ominous."

"Not meant to. Just that the individual hasn't actually harmed you yet."

"He tried to run me over!" Ruby protested.

"Right. You should have reported that when it happened. It's a little late now."

At that point, the pregnant cop waddled in.

"The car was reported stolen three weeks ago," she said.

"He's been driving a stolen car all this time?" Ruby asked.

"Apparently," the pregnant cop shrugged.

The Honda's being hot seemed to stir their interest a little, and by the time Ruby left the station, she knew that they'd put out some sort of bulletin on the Honda and that the creep probably would be stopped at a tollbooth soon. This was reassuring.

Sort of.

18. LOST

Ruby knew that Delaware Park got a big facelift when slot machines started bringing money to the old track, but she pictured the place as grim, something like Aqueduct, with lots of cement and few trees. Instead, Delaware Park was lush and nearly as lovely as Belmont. Dark green barns stood in orderly rows, and handsome old trees shaded horses and backstretch workers as they went about the business of early afternoon chores.

Violet had asked Ann Julian to leave Ruby's name at the stable gate. The guard there directed Ruby to Ann's barn. As Ruby nosed the Mustang into a spot, Spike started wagging his tail and looking all around. Ruby had no idea how he'd be around horses, so before getting out of the car, she scooped him into her arms.

Ruby had taken only a few steps toward the barn when Ann Julian materialized. She scowled at Ruby.

"Hi, Ann," Ruby said brightly.

"That a dog?"

"This is Spike," Ruby said defensively.

"Mind he doesn't bark or get underfoot," Ann said, barely relaxing her scowl.

"I'll hold on to him," Ruby said.

"How you been? You look different," Ann commented as she led the way toward her barn office.

Ruby was always flummoxed when people told her she looked *different*. She figured it was a euphemism for *older*, or *fatter*, or something generally unflattering.

"I mean you look fit," Ann added. "I hate when people tell me I look different. I always think they mean ugly."

Ruby laughed, "Thanks for clarifying. I was actually just thinking you meant something less than flattering."

They were walking past horses stalls now, and Spike was trying to struggle out of Ruby's arms, presumably to go sniff at the baffling enormous animals. Ruby held him tightly.

Ann's office was crammed with crap. File cabinets, a desk, and a sad-looking green couch all jammed inside a small, windowless room that smelled of Murphy Oil Soap. Two broken bridles were dangling from a hook. A large feed supply store calendar hung over the desk. Ann closed the door and told Ruby she could put Spike down. The puppy eagerly explored the small room, carefully sniffing everything.

Ann glanced at a corner of the calendar, squinting as she tried to make sense of what she'd written there.

"So, your guy is working for Nancy Cooley," she said, sitting down in an office chair. "She'll hire just about anyone, that one."

"Oh?" Ruby shouldn't have been surprised that Ann had tracked Elliott down so quickly. The backstretch seemed vast to outsiders, but it functioned like a small village where secrets were few.

"Barn seventeen," Ann added. She was resting her large

callused hands over her knees, looking down at the tops of her hands as if they displeased her.

"And yeah, there's a woman with him," Ann added. "City slicker type. Heard more about her than about the guy. Good-looking woman they say."

Ruby asked after Ann's string of horses. They were almost all claimers, but she talked about them as if they were stakes horses. Ruby made the right noises for the right amount of time then told Ann she needed to go find Elliott and Jody.

"Yeah. I got a lot to do too. Good luck with whatever the hell it is you're up to," Ann said.

Ruby picked Spike back up for the walk to the car. She didn't want to, but she'd have to leave the puppy in the Mustang while she nosed around.

NANCY COOLEY was a small woman in her forties. Her graying brown hair was cut in a choppy punk do that wasn't unflattering. Her blue eyes held mischief. Ruby liked her right away.

"Yeah, I hired Elliott a few days ago," Nancy said. "He seems all right. But what are you telling me—he's in some kind of trouble?"

"No, nothing like that," Ruby said. "I'm looking for a friend of his. I think she's with him."

"The redhead," Nancy said.

"Yes, Jody Ray."

"Yeah, now *there's* trouble if I ever saw it."

"Oh?" Ruby said.

"I'm just speculating. Seems like she's on the run from something."

"Do you know where they are now?"

"Elliott's cleaning tack down the aisle." Nancy motioned in the distance. "I don't know where the redhead is. Probably he's got her locked up in his room. She didn't look well last I saw her."

"Okay if I go talk to Elliott?"

"Knock yourself out."

Ruby walked down the barn aisle, passing the horses as she did. Some had their ears forward and were interested in Ruby; others made faces and pinned their ears.

Elliott was whistling as he ran a sponge over a bridle that hung from a hook. He didn't look up from his work until Ruby was right in front of him.

"Oh," he said when he saw her.

Ruby recognized him, so she assumed he recognized her too.

"Hi, Elliott. I'm Ruby, a friend of Violet's."

Elliott looked sheepish. "Violet send you to find me?"

"No, though she *is* wondering why you took off. But I'm actually looking for Jody Ray."

"Oh," Elliott said again as he turned back to wiping the bridle down. He was a nice-looking guy. Thin but strong looking. Big dark eyes.

"She's with you, right?" Ruby asked.

"Yeah," Elliott shrugged and met Ruby's gaze. "Flame-thrower's here."

Ruby was surprised to hear him call Jody by the nickname she'd assumed was a private thing between her and Tobias.

"She's in bad shape," Elliott said. "I mean crazy." He'd stopped what he was doing and was looking right at Ruby. "I mean *bad* crazy."

"Where is she?"

"In my room." Elliott motioned toward a little green bungalow almost identical to the one he'd lived in at Belmont.

"Can I go see her?"

"It's fine with me but be careful. She was violent last night."

"Violent?" Ruby was getting seriously alarmed now.

"I told you. She's bad crazy."

"Okay," Ruby said. "Thanks."

Elliott shrugged.

Ruby walked over to the bungalow and put her ear to the door. She didn't hear anything. She knocked.

Nothing happened.

She knocked again.

"Elliott's not here," a muffled voice finally said.

It was her. Ruby was relieved.

"Jody, open up. It's me, Ruby."

The silence was thick.

"Jody?" Ruby called out. "I need to talk."

"Ruby?" Jody's voice sounded weak.

"Yeah, can you open the door?"

"Just a minute," Jody said, barely audible.

It was more than a minute. A lot more. As Ruby listened to the muffled sounds of Jody rustling around, she started worrying about Spike locked inside the Mustang. It wasn't too hot a day, and she'd left the windows open a few inches, but still, she didn't like leaving him alone. Someone might break into her car to steal him. He was that cute.

"Jody?" Ruby ventured after three or four minutes had passed. Nothing. Ruby was about to knock again when the door opened a crack.

If Ruby hadn't known the face belonged to Jody, she never would have recognized her psychiatrist. The once-lustrous red hair was dull and snarled. The face was so puffy the features were blurred. The vivid blue eyes were barely visible under swollen red lids.

"Why are you here?" Jody whispered. She hadn't opened the door more than a crack.

"Tobias asked me to find you."

"What does he want?" Jody was blinking wildly, as if she hadn't seen daylight in weeks.

"To know you're okay, for one. Can I come in?"

"I'm not okay and I've had enough."

"Enough of what?" Ruby asked.

"Enough of people bothering me."

"Just let me come in for a minute," Ruby insisted. It wasn't like her to insist, to infiltrate someone's hideous private moment like this. But Jody looked bad off.

Jody slowly opened the door, moving aside enough to let Ruby squeeze through. She was wearing stained light blue pajamas and athletic socks. She closed the door after Ruby, went right to the bed, and got under the covers.

The dark green walls didn't exactly cheer the place—and

it wasn't a hotbed of cheer to begin with. There was snarled dirty clothing and take-out containers. The only light came from an incongruously large TV tuned to The Weather Channel.

"Mind if I sit?" Ruby asked, motioning at the lone chair in the place, a metal folding chair with clothing draped over the back.

"Go for it," Jody said.

Go for it?

"Why did you come here?" Jody asked. She kept looking past Ruby.

Ruby turned her head to see what was so fascinating. The only thing there was a sink. She sat down and tried to get Jody to meet her gaze.

"Jody," Ruby said softly, "what are you doing here? What's all this about?" She motioned at the dingy room. "You've run away from home? With Violet's groom?"

"I'm very tired," Jody said.

"Aren't you embarrassed?" Ruby had pulled her chair a little closer.

"Embarrassed? About what?" Jody cocked an eyebrow. It was the first sign of animation Ruby had seen.

"About me seeing you like this?"

"I look that bad?"

"I've seen you look better."

At first this seemed to worry Jody. Then she shrugged slightly and pulled the covers all the way up to her chin. She looked like a psychotic twelve-year-old.

"What does Toby want me for?"

"He's worried about you."

"He wants some money. That's more like it," Jody said it resentfully. "Do you know how tired I am of all this?"

Ruby decided she wouldn't even try to answer that. "Tobias paid me to find you, and I needed money so I did it. Now I've found you. I'll tell him where you are. He really is worried about you," Ruby said.

"Yes. Everyone has always been worried about me," Jody said, running her hand over her forehead as if brushing a fever away. "And I'm tired of that too."

Ruby wondered if there was anything Jody wasn't tired of. Then she got back to worrying about Spike. The dog had been confined for twenty minutes now.

"Are you a dog person?" she asked Jody.

"What?"

"I have a dog. A puppy. I just got him. He's locked in my car. I'm worried about him. Can I bring him in here?"

Jody blinked. Her mouth opened slightly then closed again. She was resting her hands outside the covers now, and Ruby saw that the cuticles had been bitten raw.

"Sure," Jody shrugged, "bring the puppy, yes."

Ruby rose from the metal chair. "I'll be back in two minutes," she told her, wondering if Jody would let her back in.

Ruby walked back around Nancy Cooley's shed row to where she'd parked the Mustang. She was dazed and a little light-headed. She didn't want to think about what she'd just found in the bungalow, about the demise of a woman Ruby had trusted to be stable, steady, and constant. It was almost funny.

Spike acted as though he hadn't seen Ruby in months. He licked and wiggled and bounced. Ruby snapped the leash on and tried to get him to walk at her side. He kept running ahead, nearly pulling Ruby's shoulder from its socket. A hotwalker was leading a horse by, and Ruby looked down to see if Spike was going to bark or scare the horse. The puppy dropped down to his belly, flattening himself out submissively for what he thought was a giant, dominant dog. The horse walked by. Spike slowly got up and stared after it.

Ruby knocked at Jody's door. No answer.

"Jody? I'm coming in." Ruby turned the doorknob. It wasn't locked. As she opened the door and walked in, Spike bounded forward into the room.

Jody Ray was standing in the middle of the small room, her soiled pajamas were hanging off her, her hair was in her face, and she was laughing hysterically.

19. FLAMETHROWER

Jody was so skinny the laughter shook her body like wind through a bag of sticks. Excited by the laughter, Spike ran over and jumped on Jody, putting his front paws on her thighs.

"Spike, off," Ruby yelled. Jody looked whacko enough to do something bad to the dog.

"I'm not going to hurt him," Jody said sharply. The laughter was all gone, and she let herself collapse backwards on the bed. One of her pajama pant legs was hiked up over her knee, and Ruby saw leg hair. She'd stopped shaving her legs. This more than anything indicated Jody's state of mind. She wasn't the hairy-legged type.

"Why do people call you Flamethrower?" Ruby heard herself ask. She hadn't known it was coming.

"Where did you hear that?" Jody sat forward a little and was trying to focus her eyes.

"Tobias. And Elliott mentioned it too."

"Oh." She lay back against the pillow. "It was a stripping name."

"A what?"

"My dancing name. When I was a stripper."

"What, was every woman under the age of fifty a stripper at some point?"

"Very possibly." Jody actually smiled. "Just another part of my troubled adolescence. And I seem to remember your having had a brief stripping career yourself."

"A miserable failure," Ruby shrugged. She felt a little easier now. They were talking, like old times, Jody remembering particulars of Ruby's past. The thing that was different was Jody revealing herself.

"How did they come to call you Flamethrower at a strip club?"

"I'd dated the manager," Jody shrugged. "He'd called me that long before I'd taken my clothes off for money. I suppose he found me passionate." She smiled a small smile. "Later, Millie, one of my female lovers, came up with the very same nickname without my ever having told her. She said I was always generating heat." Jody's eyes had milked over now, and she seemed to be in another world. "Then of course there was Flamethrower the horse. That attractive chestnut colt. I followed his career with interest. Poor Millie," Jody continued, "poor all of them. I savaged them. You know the way they describe a stud colt as *savaging* other horses?" Jody looked at Ruby.

Ruby nodded slightly.

"I think you could say the same of me."

"Oh," said Ruby. She really didn't want to hear this. "I actually met Millie," she changed the subject.

"You did?" Jody's eyes focused.

"She told me about your place in Trout Falls. I went there looking for you."

"You did?" Jody's eyes were big and round now.

"Yeah."

"You've gone to a lot of trouble."

"Sort of, yes."

"That was kind of you," Jody said. "Did you see Dolly?"

"Yes, she was there."

"She's been through hell," Jody said. "Two husbands died in front of her."

"She mentioned one."

"There were two. The first was a violent death. A holdup in a liquor store in Philly. Poor Dolly was right there."

"That's awful," said Ruby.

"It was. I suspect her body went haywire as a result. The fatness I mean. She wasn't always that way. I think she had to grow a protective layer."

"Uh" was all Ruby could muster.

"Don't you go doing that sort of thing."

"Eating myself to death?"

"No, I can't imagine your taking that particular path. But whatever. Drinking. What have you. None of it helps." Jody suddenly fell back on the pillows, exhausted. She closed her eyes.

Ruby let the silence be.

"What's that smell?" Jody asked after several minutes.

"What?"

"Are you smoking?" Jody sat up.

"No," said Ruby.

"Something's burning." Jody sniffed at the air.

Ruby smelled it then. "What is that?"

"It's coming from up there." Jody pointed toward the roof. "Oh," she added blandly, "smoke."

Ruby looked up and saw black smoke feathering in from where the roof met the top of the walls.

"Shit. Let's get out of here," said Ruby. She picked Spike up off the floor.

Jody was staring at the smoke, not showing any signs of stirring.

"Jody? Come on, we should go." There was brown smoke mingling with the gray smoke now, and Ruby could hear something crackling.

Jody looked all around but still didn't get up.

"Come on." Holding Spike with one arm, Ruby grabbed one of her psychiatrist's hands and started pulling.

"I'll be right with you," Jody said in a small voice. "Just go on." She waved Ruby away.

"I'm not going to leave you in here. It's getting too smoky. It's dangerous. Come on."

"I said I'll be right with you. I have to fix myself. I look like shit."

Ruby was torn. She didn't want to leave Jody behind, but she didn't want Spike breathing in smoke either.

"All right, but hurry up," Ruby said. She opened the door and rushed out. A few feet away from the bungalow, she turned back and looked. The whole roof was engulfed in flames. Nearby, people were pointing and yelling. Some had taken out cell phones.

Ruby put Spike down and went back to the front door of

the bungalow. "Jody," she called. "It's bad, come on, get out."
Ruby was about to open the door and go back in when there
was a huge explosion of heat. Ruby took several steps backwards then tripped and fell, landing on her ass. Next thing she
knew, she was staring at a smoldering piece of roofing, and
Spike was licking her face. All around, people were shouting.
The bungalow's roof had caved in. Ruby felt someone lifting
her by the armpits. She was dragged back a few hundred feet,
and someone shoved a metal chair under her just before she
collapsed. She found she was clutching Spike's leash, and the
dog was there, looking at her, confused.

Within a matter of seconds, fire extinguishers were being
pointed at the blaze, but they had no effect.

It seemed like an eternity before two fire trucks and then
an ambulance appeared. It was only then that Ruby realized
Jody could not have survived.

Ruby vomited.

———

ANN JULIAN appeared and knelt down in front of Ruby.

"Who can I call for you?" she was asking.

Ruby shook her head. There wasn't anyone to call.

"Can you get my dog some water?" she heard herself
asking.

"Sure," Ann said. She turned and melted off into the
distance.

Other people came forward. Nancy Cooley. A female
security guard. Then Elliott. His lips were drawn and bluish,
and his eyes took up most of his face.

"She wouldn't come out?"

Ruby kept shaking her head. Elliott receded.

Eventually, someone brought water for both Spike and Ruby. Then a very short cop was asking Ruby if she was hurt.

"No," Ruby murmured. "I'm fine. When can I leave?"

"Not for a while yet. I'm sorry," the cop said, "the detectives are going to need to speak with you. We need you to identify a suspect."

"Suspect?"

"Security caught some idiot trying to speed out the stable gate the wrong way. Had accelerant in his car."

"Oh," said Ruby.

Spike had crawled under the chair Ruby was sitting on. He'd stretched out and was napping comfortably. Ruby closed her eyes. Maybe she could somehow nap too.

"Ruby."

She'd actually drifted off for a few seconds, but the sound of that particular voice would have woken her from a coma. It was Ed. She stared at him, unsure if he was really there. "How did you get here?" was all she could think to ask.

"Drove."

"But how'd you know I was here?"

"Violet called me a couple of hours ago, told me what you were up to, and talked some sense into me. Ruby, I'm sorry. I had a crisis. I'm over it. But I've been an idiot."

"Yes," Ruby said, "you have." As Ruby looked up at Ed, Spike scrambled to his feet and started licking Ed's hand.

"Whose puppy?

"Mine."

"What?"

"I adopted him last night."

Ed's mouth opened half an inch, but he thought better of saying anything. He offered Ruby his hand and pulled her to her feet. As she looked up at him, he put his palms on top of her shoulders. She let him.

"Could we take you over to the security office now to identify a suspect?" A cop had come over.

"I didn't see anyone, but sure, I'll look," Ruby said.

"Apparently you filed a complaint about this individual."

Ruby was so dazed it took her a few seconds to put two and two together and realize it was her stalker.

She was glad Ed was with her as she walked into the small security office. One of the guards gave Spike a funny look but said nothing.

The black-haired guy she'd seen behind the wheel of the Honda so many times was sitting in a chair with his hands handcuffed behind him.

"Ruby Murphy," he said, apparently unfazed by the fact that there were cops everywhere. "You don't remember me, do you?" He stared at her. His eyes were cold blue marbles.

"Am I supposed to?"

"When you fuck up someone's life, you should remember. Least, that's the way I see it."

In one awful moment, Ruby realized who he was.

"Frank," she said. He had dyed his hair and lost some weight, but it was him. The one-time boyfriend and associate of Ariel DiCello, an unstable woman who had hired Ruby to find out that Frank was not only cheating on her but was a for-hire horse assassin as well. After the whole unpleasant thing had come to a head and the Feds had stepped in, Frank had been convicted of fraud and shipped off to prison. What he was doing out already, Ruby couldn't imagine. Nor did she understand why he was holding her to blame.

"I've been waiting for this." Frank narrowed his eyes.

"Waiting for what?"

"To get revenge."

"I didn't do anything," Ruby said.

Ed was standing right by Ruby's side, speechless. Even the cop who'd escorted them over seemed fascinated and was letting Frank babble on.

"That's not how I see it," he said. "Now you know what it feels like."

"What what feels like?"

"To lose everything you value. To live in fear. To have everyone doubt everything you say and do."

"You sent those pictures to Ed?"

"Sure." Frank actually smiled.

"And you stole money from the museum?" She asked, keeping an eye on the gun.

"Couldn't resist."

"How'd you get in there?"

"Paid my admission like everyone else. You were sitting right there at the register."

Ruby felt her mouth opening and closing. She'd been doing a lot of that lately.

"You were the guy who told me the trash was on fire?"

"Yes." Frank smiled even wider, proud of his work.

Ruby remembered wondering about the weird-looking bearded man at the museum a few weeks back. He'd told her the bathroom trash was on fire. She'd gone in to find a cigarette butt smoldering in the wastebasket and had wondered if the guy who'd told her about it had actually been responsible. Then figured that was silly. But Frank had done it. He'd started a fire, drawn her away from the register, and apparently pilfered the large bills Bob kept stashed underneath the cash drawer.

"Why?"

"You fucked up my life."

"All I did was tell someone else about some of the things you were doing."

"It wasn't any of your business. Now you know what it's like having someone meddle in your business, don't you? It's not that pleasant, is it? You feel like you're going to snap, right?"

"How did you find me here?" Ruby felt she might be pressing her luck with the twenty-questions routine, but she needed all the facts.

"The wonders of modern technology. GPS tracking system. Slapped one on that pretty little Mustang of yours."

By now, two more cops had crammed into the security office, and one of them, a detective, stepped in.

"All right, miss, so this is the guy?"

"Yeah," Ruby nodded. She felt numb and sick.

"Go on outside. I'll finish up here and tell them what we know about Frank," Ed said, gently guiding Ruby and Spike to the door.

"Okay," Ruby nodded.

Outside, she leaned back against the wall of the office, then slowly sank down to the ground. Spike licked her cheek.

———

BY THE TIME ED walked Ruby back to Nancy Cooley's shed row, where he'd parked his car, the fire had been brought under control, and the firefighters were slowly pulling back the charred pieces of bungalow. As Ruby stood there, gaping, she saw a leg, disembodied and blackened. Ruby thought it a particularly sick irony that the last thing she should see of her psychiatrist was a leg, detached from the body it had once supported.

Ruby vomited again.

"Come on, you don't need to see this," Ed said. Nancy Cooley had appeared and now ushered Ruby, Ed, and Spike into her barn office.

"Sit," Nancy said solicitously.

Ruby let herself collapse backwards onto a chair.

———

RUBY DECIDED SHE would make Ed jump through quite a few hoops before she'd forgive him, but he did make her life a whole lot easier over the next few hours. He could talk the talk with all the law enforcement officials, and he monitored the people questioning Ruby.

Ruby had just finished giving her statement to yet another official and was alone in Nancy's office when her cell phone rang, the ominous *unidentified caller* showing up on the screen. She guessed it was Tobias. She braced herself.

"Yes?"

"Hello, Ruby," Tobias said.

"Jody is dead." Ruby came right out with it.

"Excuse me?"

"Your wife died in a fire." Ruby didn't see what use it would be prettying up an ugly fact.

There was a long, awful silence.

"How?" he finally asked.

"It's partially my fault. I was being stalked. My stalker set the bungalow on fire," Ruby said.

"Bungalow?"

"Where Jody was staying. I was in there talking to her. The guy set the place on fire."

Ruby was having trouble making complete sentences. She stuttered out the rest of it. How she couldn't get Jody to leave the bungalow. How the roof collapsed. She left out the part about the leg.

"She thought she looked bad." Ruby couldn't get this out of her head. How Jody apparently had died because she didn't want the world to see her looking like shit. "She wanted to brush her hair or something."

Tobias kept falling into long silences, and Ruby would gently remind him she was there, at the other end of the line.

"What did you tell the police about me?" he eventually asked in a small, resigned-sounding voice.

"I gave them your home phone number since you're next of kin."

"You didn't tell them?"

"That you were trying to extort your wife for money? No.

221

I didn't see the point. She's dead. You lost a leg. That has to be enough."

"The cops won't be looking for me?"

"Only to notify you about your wife."

There was another long silence.

"I have to go now," Ruby said.

"Yes," Tobias said. "All right."

Ruby squeezed her puppy to her chest. He licked her chin.

20. PARADISE

It was hot for mid-September, the mercury tickling 95 and a huge low-slung sun casting haze over Belmont.

Ruby locked herself inside Violet's office so she could change her clothes in privacy. Spike jumped onto the ancient office couch, spun around in two circles, then plopped down and closed his eyes, immediately falling asleep. Ruby envied him.

She took the crazy pink and white seersucker dress out of the suit bag. She'd bought it a week earlier on a shopping expedition with Jane, who'd finally come back from India. They'd had a restorative afternoon together, spending money on frivolous items and cheering each other up. Jane was recovering from hideous intestinal parasites she'd gotten in India, and Ruby was taking baby steps toward feeling less skittish and haunted. Buying the absurd pink and white dress helped. Only now she had to wear the damned thing. Juan the Bullet was making his debut in a little more than an hour, and Ruby had to sit in a box with the owners. She had to look festive.

There was a knock at the door, and Ruby's heart missed a few beats. She was still nervous all the time, jumping at the slightest sound. She figured it would be like this for a while.

"Ruby?" It was Violet.

"Just a minute." Ruby zipped up the dress. She'd had to

change in Violet's office since Ed had banished her while he got Juan the Bullet ready—banished her gently and apologetically the way he did most things with her lately, but banished.

Ruby opened the door to let Violet in.

"Oh!" Violet seemed genuinely shocked. "You look fantastic!"

"I don't look like a drag queen?"

"Stop being ridiculous."

"Okay," Ruby shrugged.

"They're here again," Violet said, lowering her voice.

"Who?"

"Tobias and Miller."

"Oh," said Ruby.

In some convoluted version of Stockholm syndrome, Tobias and his kidnapper, Elvin Miller, had become bizarrely inseparable. Tobias didn't have any business at the track, but a few days after Jody's death he started turning up at Violet's barn to stare forlornly at the horses he didn't own. Violet didn't have the heart to ban Tobias, but having him around made her nervous. What's more, Miller, whose job it was to navigate the wheelchair through thoroughly inaccessible areas of the backstretch, was a reckless driver and sometimes spooked the horses.

"Will you say hello? Tell them Juan the Bullet is racing?"

"Won't that make Tobias feel shittier?" Ruby asked.

"I think it would cheer him up."

"Okay," Ruby shrugged again.

"I'll see you in the clubhouse later?"

Ruby nodded. She snapped Spike's lead onto his collar then walked out into the barn aisle, taking care not to step in a puddle with her new bright green sandals, repeatedly chiding Spike, who kept trying to make a beeline for the manure pile.

As she came around the corner at the end of the barn, Ruby nearly collided with Tobias's wheelchair.

"Sorry, Ruby," Tobias said. "My driver is drunk." He motioned at Miller, who looked glum but not drunk. Tobias had been given a prosthesis, but he seemed to prefer having Miller wheel him around.

"Good luck with Juan the Bullet," Tobias said.

"Oh, you know?"

"Part of why we're here. Wanted to watch the race live." He looked slightly sad saying it. Fearless Jones, whose new owners had put him with a trainer in California, had sustained a career-ending ligament injury. He would recover but would never race again. There wouldn't be any bittersweet thrills for Tobias watching the horse he'd lost turn into a stakes winner.

"Good luck," Tobias said, "and tell Ed good luck too."

"Thanks," said Ruby. "Nice to see you," she added, even though she wasn't sure it was.

As she watched Miller wheeling Tobias away, Ruby wondered what Jody would think of her husband now. Ruby thought about Jody at least once a day, had added the psychiatrist to the repertoire of dead people she sometimes imagined were watching her. It was harrowing but better, she supposed, than not thinking about it at all and internalizing it till it turned into a neurosis that one day would come screaming out at the wrong time.

Ruby walked back over to Ed's barn to lock Spike in the

office until after Juan's race. The puppy stared at her long and hard then rested his head on his paws and sighed.

Ruby didn't run into Ed, who was probably at the security barn with Juan. She made her way to the clubhouse to look for the owners.

———

THE HEAT HADN'T kept the fans away. Belmont was unusually crowded for a Friday in fall. There were women in hats, aging patriarchs in navy blue suits, girls in skimpy outfits, and, here and there, bedraggled degenerate gambler types grumbling about the heat and the crowd.

It was fifteen minutes to post time, and Ruby was standing with Juan the Bullet's owners, Lisa and Mary Tyson. Ruby's dress was itchy, and her shoes pinched her feet as she stood inside the leafy Belmont paddock. Juan was in his saddling stall, shaking his head as Ed put the saddle on and Nicky tightened the girth.

The paddock judge called "Riders up," and Nicky led Juan the Bullet from his saddling stall. Ed gave the rider, Freddy Frio, a leg up.

"Oh, he's so beautiful," Lisa said softly.

"Yes," Ruby agreed, "he is." She was admiring Ed as much as the horse though. Ed looked particularly good to her right then. In the month since Jody's death, Ed had cooked dinner repeatedly, bought at least six dozen roses, and frequently thrown Ruby down on the bed for the kind of impromptu frenzied screwing she liked best. So Ed looked good. But the horse did too. Juan was still pigeon-toed and a little underweight, but, at that moment, under the giant sun, with his tack gleaming and his tiny rider astride, Juan the Bullet was magnificent.

As the horses were led to the track to meet up with their ponies, Ed came over to attempt to exude confidence for Mary and Lisa's benefit. Ruby knew it wasn't entirely an act. He believed Juan the Bullet had a much better chance than his 34–1 odds might indicate.

"I'll be watching from the rail," Ed told the two women. He'd already warned them he'd be too agitated to sit in their box. It was Ruby's job to make sure Mary and Lisa were comfortable and entertained.

"See you in the winner's circle." Mary winked at Ed.

Ed offered a weak smile.

While Lisa went to sit in the box, Mary and Ruby headed for the betting lines. Ruby was in line right behind Mary and heard the woman putting a thousand dollars to win on Juan. Ruby didn't want to risk the racing gods' wrath by making an enormous bet on her boyfriend's horse. She kept it to twenty dollars to win.

Ruby tried to relax as she settled into her seat next to Lisa, but her stomach was knotted and she felt like her eyes were bulging out of her head. She noticed that Mary and Lisa had a bottle of champagne in an ice bucket. She sincerely hoped they'd have a reason to pop it.

Out on the track, Juan was on his toes, ears flicking slightly in response to his rider's hands. While the other two-year-olds nervously danced and crow-hopped, Juan arched his neck and focused. He looked like a pro. His chestnut coat gleamed red under the sun, and for a second, Ruby flashed on Jody's vividly red hair. It would be a long time before she stopped seeing that awful picture of her psychiatrist's charred, disembodied leg. But at least Ruby had stopped seeing Attila's lifeless head, his blood staining her fingers. That, she had come to terms with. Finally.

Ruby's stomach flipped as the horses loaded into the starting gate. Juan went in and stood solidly on all fours with his ears pricked forward.

The bell rang, the gates opened, and nine maiden colts and geldings popped out. Juan the Bullet broke well and shot to the lead. His strides were short but machine-gun quick. He opened a two-length lead on the others. Ruby felt her stomach twist up even more. The race was only seven-eighths of a mile, and front-runners won those often enough, but Ruby would have preferred to see the little chestnut tucked into second or third, stalking the pace. The jockey was skiing in the irons, trying to hold Juan back, but it wasn't doing much good. Juan wasn't rank per se, he had his ears forward and looked very cheerful, but he was insisting on having it all his way.

Though the horses behind him kept shifting positions and taking turns coming up to Juan the Bullet's hind end, it looked as though Juan was on his own magic carpet. No one seemed to be able to get all the way up to threaten him.

As they came around the turn, Ruby watched the rider finally give Juan the Bullet his head. The little colt put his ears forward and surged. At the same time, the number-five horse, a big bay, broke away from the pack and came neck and neck with Juan. Ruby watched Juan pin his ears, threatening his opponent. The jockey showed Juan the whip but didn't touch him with it. Juan surged monstrously and, in a few seconds, had three lengths on the bay. Ruby held her breath. There was only an eighth of a mile to go, but she'd seen it time and again: tiring front-runners looking for a place to lie down as the closers came on to collect the pieces.

She needn't have worried. Juan the Bullet expanded his lead by another length and cruised home by daylight. His ears were forward.

Ruby's legs had stopped working, and she had to sit down. She couldn't feel her extremities. Next thing she knew, Lisa was grabbing hold of her, pulling her to her feet and down the stairs toward the winner's circle. There was a blur of smiling faces, and then Ed was hugging Ruby and saying, "We did it! We did it!"

Nicky the groom was grinning broadly, and Violet, who had suddenly materialized, was kissing everyone, including Mary and Lisa. Only Juan the Bullet stood primly still, his head held high, almost disdainful as the track photographer documented the happy event. Lisa and Mary took turns kissing their horse's nose before Nicky led him out of the winner's circle and back toward the barn.

"Come to the box to celebrate." Mary gestured to include Ed, Ruby, and Violet.

Mary popped the champagne, and diminutive Lisa lit a big cigar. Violet, who, as far as Ruby knew, had met Mary and Lisa only once, had her arm looped through Mary's and was regaling the strapping blonde with the story of one of her horses who manured in his water bucket when something displeased him.

By her third glass of champagne, Lisa had befriended a pair of brunettes in the next box over. The ladies were all working on another bottle of champagne when Ed and Ruby left them.

"They're happy," Ed commented as he and Ruby headed back to the stable area.

"Deliriously," Ruby said. She was walking gingerly so as not to stain the sandals that were killing her feet.

"And you?" Ed said.

"And me what?"

"Are you happy? Delirious? We never talk about it. About your state of mind."

This was true. Ruby never mentioned the aftermath of having been stalked or of feeling responsible for not dragging Jody out of the bungalow.

"Oh," Ruby said, "I'm fine. Frank's not getting out for the next few decades."

"I meant Jody. You don't still feel responsible, do you?"

"No, I'm all right with it. I'm fine," Ruby said, even though this wasn't entirely true.

"What does 'fine' mean in this instance?"

"It means fine. I'm glad you and I are good, and I'm glad to have my job back. But I do feel fucked up about Jody's death. Like that."

"That's what I mean. You feel fucked up. Are you going to be all right?"

"Do you mean should I go see a psychiatrist to deal with

my own psychiatrist having let herself burn to death? No. Probably not." Ruby felt her shoulders tense.

Ed smiled slightly. "Okay, okay. Don't get worked up."

"I'm not," Ruby shrugged. They'd reached Ed's shed row, and Ruby couldn't wait to liberate Spike from the office.

"You're going to The Hole now?"

"In a minute, yeah. I'm gonna change clothes and get Spike. Then go."

Ed put his hands on her hips and looked down into her, deep into her.

"You okay?"

"Not bad."

"I got you something."

"Something?"

"A present."

"Really?"

Ed walked down the aisle a few paces and opened one of the tack trunks there.

"Here," he said, handing Ruby a cloth sack.

"What is it?"

"Look inside and see."

Ruby opened the sack and pulled out two beautiful pieces of leather. There was a collar with a brass plaque reading SPIKE and a lovely leash as well.

"These are beautiful!" Ruby practically screamed.

"Had the bridle maker make them," Ed said, "that guy down in Maryland. Spike will look good in that."

Ruby thought fleetingly of the vegan Goth girl at the pet store in Trout Falls and repressed a smile. "Thank you, Ed, thank you." She reached up, pulled his head closer, and kissed him vigorously.

He dug his fingers into the small of her back.

"I'll see you at home," Ruby said.

She felt his eyes on her ass as she walked over to the office door.

Spike jumped off the couch and wiggled. He was going at it so hard it was a struggle putting his new collar on. Once Ruby did get the collar on though, it was a thing of beauty. Spike looked like a million bucks. Ruby picked him up, which wasn't easy. He was pushing fifty pounds now. She let him lick her cheek then put him down and closed the office door so she could change into barn clothes. Spike started bouncing off the walls, jumping onto the couch then off again, looking at Ruby and making little whining noises in his throat in case she had any doubts about his needing a good long romp.

Ruby took her hair down and looked at herself in the tiny mirror hanging to the right of Ed's desk. The facial bruising was long gone, but there were dark circles under her eyes, and her face was narrow and pale. Ruby had never been a rosy-cheeked corn-fed type, but right now she looked nearly cadaverous. She really hadn't been eating, riding her bike, or doing much yoga. The only time she moved her body was when she hoisted herself up onto Jack Valentine's back every few days to trot around the paddock. She wondered how long she'd looked like this and why no one had said anything.

"Ugh," she said aloud.

Spike tilted his head and looked at her.

"I don't always look like this," Ruby said.

The dog tilted his head the other way.

Ruby was supposed to be at The Hole by 5 P.M. to help Coleman with the kids who were coming for a horsemanship lesson. And Bob, who'd been afraid to do anything other than be nice and grovel for several weeks, had dared to ask Ruby to stop by the museum later to help him sort through slides for a history of Coney Island lecture. Elsie wanted Ruby to look through a baby-naming book with her that night. And there were probably a half dozen other things she was supposed to do too. But it could wait. All of it.

Ruby drove with the windows down, letting the wind cool her. Spike was squinting, the wind flapping his ears. Ruby got onto the Belt Parkway but got off before the exit to The Hole. She pulled the Mustang into the parking area for one of the small beaches just off the Belt. Spike trotted next to her as she walked down the sandy path to the water of Jamaica Bay. It was ten degrees cooler here, and a strong wind masked the traffic sounds.

The little beach was completely deserted, and the water lapping at the white sand was a brilliant blue. It was a pocket of unexpected paradise, a tiny slice of beauty at the edge of the world.

Ruby picked up a stick of driftwood and threw it for Spike. He bounded ahead, retrieved the stick, and deposited it at Ruby's feet. He looked from Ruby to the stick and back. He tilted his head. Ruby threw the stick again.

There was a figure walking toward Ruby, coming from

the other end of the beach. As the figure came closer, Ruby saw it was a homeless-looking guy. His clothes were dirty rags, and he was barefoot.

"Good afternoon," he said formally as he came within a few feet of Ruby.

"Hello," said Ruby.

The man smiled. He had perfect teeth.

"Do you have a cigarette?" he asked.

Ruby fished her pack out from her jeans pocket.

"Here, I don't need them," she said, offering the whole pack.

The guy looked surprised then quickly pocketed the pack, secreting it into one of the folds of his clothing.

"Thank you, lady, thank you," he said. He walked past Ruby.

Above, two gulls hovered, as if dangling from strings a ghost had thrown through the sky.

Ruby found a Fireball in her pocket and popped it into her mouth.

ABOUT THE AUTHOR

MAGGIE ESTEP is the author of six books and her first crime novel, *Hex,* was a *New York Times* Notable Book of 2003. Her writing has appeared in many magazines and anthologies, including *Brooklyn Noir, The Best American Erotica,* and *Hard Boiled Brooklyn.* Maggie is the co-editor of *Bloodlines: An Anthology of Horse Racing.* She lives in Brooklyn, New York.

For more information, go to www.maggieestep.com.

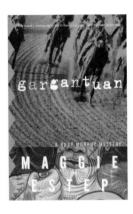